DEATH ON THE HALF SHELL

The Possumwood Mysteries Book 2

HOLLY DEY

DEATH
ON THE
HALF SHELL

The Possumwood Mysteries Book 2

HOLLY DEY

ISBN: 978-1-941502-09-9

ISBN 978-1-941502-09-9

Acknowledgements

I couldn't do this without the love and support of my wonderful family. I love you so much!

Chapter 1

PRIMROSE CORVINA DONOVAN, who preferred to go by PC, bent her elbow and adjusted her aim. She closed one eye, then the other, but that didn't help much. She flicked her wrist and let the dart fly.

"It's in!" Jim Hargraves' voice bellowed across the room.

"It can't be!" his wife, Winnie, argued. She stepped up and squinted at the dartboard. "It's in. Barely."

"We are the champions," crooned Drew Berlusconi. "Raptors buy the next round."

PC looked at her watch. "I've got to get home and make sure Mama took her meds. See you next week." She waved at the small group of people sipping craft beer in the dartboard area.

She had been reluctant to accept when Drew had invited her to meet up with the Wednesday Night Regulars at the Biersal Brew Pub for a game of darts. But she'd enjoyed it enough the first time that she came back for a second round this week.

Her mother, Rose, lived just over a mile from downtown Possumwood. Rocky, PC's brother, was at home, so he could help if Rose needed anything. She'd just had hip replacement surgery, and PC was staying with her to take care of her menagerie of rescue farm animals. It was a good thing she'd just retired after twenty-five years as a homicide detective, because now she had plenty of time to help Rose while she recuperated.

It was a pleasant break to get out of the house for a little bit, and PC didn't mind walking, so she could have a drink or two with friends. Or acquaintances, as the case may be. Darts... was fun. The people were friendly, and the games were low-key, more about visiting than competing. Although Winnie Hargraves, who had gone to school with her mother, could hit the bullseye almost every time.

Still, PC missed going out to a spontaneous dinner with her friends back in Houston. Or the theatre. She loved the Alley, even though she hadn't had a lot of time to take in plays while she was working.

PC finished putting away her borrowed darts and slid the case across the table to Drew. He got up and walked her to the door of the cavernous bar. "So, were you planning on going to brunch on Sunday?"

"Yes."

He paused, seemingly surprised by her answer.

"I'm driving my mother and her friends to Valentine's brunch. Terribly romantic, I know. But they go every year."

"Then I'll probably see you there."

"I believe they're all planning to wear red hats, so we'll be easy to spot. We should get there around 10:30."

PC leaned on the door and it opened a few inches, letting in a chilly breeze.

"You know, I'd be happy to give you a lift home, so you aren't out walking in the dark and cold."

"Drew, it's okay. It's not that cold, and I need a little PT, anyway."

"Pacific Time?"

"Physical Training. See you on Sunday. Good night." She stepped out onto the covered porch and pushed the door closed behind her.

Since she had come back to Possumwood, PC had struggled to work in her usual morning run. Getting Rocky off the hook for a murder he didn't commit right off the bat didn't help. But now that she'd been here almost a month, her schedule had mostly fallen into place. She pulled the headlamp out of her coat pocket, snugged the band around her head, and switched it on.

PC walked the first block, then broke into a jog. She made it home in less than ten minutes, feeling good from the exertion.

Her brother was flopped on the couch watching TV. PC's terrier mix, Cordite, lay next to Rocky. The dog's tail thumped against the sofa when she came in, but that was his only reaction.

"Mama already gone to bed?"

"Yeah."

"Do you know if she took all her pills?"

Rocky shrugged. "She took *some* pills. Don't know if it was all of them."

She checked the pill sorter box. This evening's medications were gone.

"I don't suppose anyone's taken Cordite out to pee?"

Rocky scratched under the dog's chin. "Not my dog."

"Cordie, you need to pee-pee?"

The wiry-haired dog stretched, then jumped off the couch and looked at her expectantly.

PC found the leash and snapped it onto his collar. May as well check on her mother's small menagerie while she was out in the back yard. The chickens were already closed into their coop, and it would be more trouble than it was worth to look in on them. She checked the animals bedded down in the big pen. Guinevere, the caramel-colored donkey, flicked a comically oversized ear toward PC. Arthur, the much darker one-eyed jack, lay snoozing in the shavings, legs folded against his body. Hazel, the tripod goat, snuggled next to him.

"No opening the gate, Miss Gwen. You hear me?"

The donkey made a little "Ahem" sound.

"Good night."

Cordite didn't bother the chickens, and had better sense than to harass the donkeys, so PC usually let him run loose in the paddock while she was feeding and mucking out the barn in the mornings.

"Cordie! Time to go inside. C'mon!"

The little beige dog sidled up to her, making sure she only saw the left side of his body. But before he got close, she could smell it.

"Ugh! What did you get into? That is rank."

He tried to turn away from her, but she made him sit. He hung his head as she studied the dark streaks on his left shoulder. "Is that... poop?" She put her hands on her hips and scowled at the dog, who laid himself on the ground and rolled over onto his back. "You know what? You need a haircut anyway."

She got out her phone and did a quick search.

"Possumwood Animal Clinic. How may I help you?"

4

"Yes. My name is PC Donovan, and my dog's rolled in something nasty. Is there any way someone could bathe him and give him a trim today?"

"The groomer has a slot open at two o'clock. How big is your dog?"

"Twenty-ish pounds. He mostly needs a trim around his face—hair's getting in his eyes. Can I bring him now? He reeks, and I can't let him in my mama's house coated in poop. Or whatever that is."

"Sure, but he won't be ready until after three."

"That's fine. See you soon."

"Mama? I'm going to run some errands. You need anything while I'm out?"

"Can I give you my shoppin' list, honey?"

"Sure."

PC tucked the notebook paper into her pocket. She also grabbed two trash bags, the leash, and her car keys. Her mother gave her a quizzical look, but PC continued out to the RAV4 as if making a seat cover out of leaf-n-lawn bags was the most normal thing in the world.

A cold front had dropped the temperature into the upper forties, but she drove across town to the vet clinic with the windows down a few inches so she could breathe. As the mess on Cordite's side dried, it got slightly less stinky. But not enough to roll up the windows.

PC filled out the new patient form after the tech took the stink bomb of a dog into the back. The receptionist gave her a big smile. Then her jaw clenched, and she coughed.

"Abike's fantastic with all the animals. She'll take good care of…" she glanced at the form, "Cordite. Come any time after three, but we close at six. Board is $25 per night if you don't pick him up in time."

"Thanks." PC gestured to a door with male and female stylized silhouettes. "You mind if I wash my hands?"

"Be my guest!"

It took three rounds of scrubbing with anti-bacterial soap to get the funk off. PC didn't envy the groomer.

The detective stopped at the City Café for a bite to eat. It was eleven o'clock–too late for breakfast, too early for lunch. She got a cup of coffee and a slice of cherry pie, then stared out the window, musing about her to-do list. By the time she went to the feed store and did her mother's shopping, she'd probably still have a little time to kill before picking up a hopefully freshly fluffed and deodorized dog.

PC packed the groceries in among the bags of feed and closed the liftgate. A glance at her watch showed she still had an hour and a half before she could pick up Cordite. For a moment, she resisted the idea of dropping off groceries, then running all the way back across town to get the dog. *Across town… what is that, a mile? Two, at most? Besides, you have some frozen stuff.*

In the end, she went home to unpack everything, then chatted with Rose before going to pick up her freshly fumigated pooch.

Cordite was so happy to be back home that he snorted and rolled all over the floor.

Rose looked around, sniffing like a dog. "Did you buy a new perfume? Smells nice."

"No, that's Cordite you smell. He's been to the groomer, and they put foo-foo spray on him."

"Well, you should try a new perfume. Might make it easier to get a man."

"Mother!"

"Valentine's Day is coming up. You should have a date for the brunch. You know, I think Drew is sweet on you—you should invite him."

"Thanks, Mama."

"Some romance would do you good. When was the last time you had a date?"

PC rubbed the bridge of her nose. "I can't believe we're even discussing this."

"You haven't dated anyone since Mike, have you?"

"Yes." PC didn't think she was lying, but she couldn't remember anyone, specifically.

Rose's brow furrowed, but she didn't ask any more about it. "How many people can you fit in your car again? We're going to get Justice, of course. And Terry. And I thought I'd ask Imogene if she wanted a ride."

"That should be fine." PC ran a hand through her hair. The name sounded familiar, but she couldn't place it. "Have I met Terry? Where does she live?"

"What makes you think Terry is a she? And yes, you have met *him*. At the art gallery? Remember now?"

This is going to be like that very first date with Woody in eighth grade when Mama drove us to the movies, then sat in between us. Except in reverse. She cringed inwardly. "Fine, Mama. Where does *he* live?"

A sly smile curled Rose's lips. "Two doors down, other side of the Youns."

"He lives two doors down, and he hasn't come to see you?" PC plopped onto the couch next to Rocky.

"You're not always around. And you're a very sound sleeper."

"Mother, are you sneaking men into your room at night? Am I going to have to take away your cell phone and put a lock on your door?"

Rocky snorted, unable to hold back a laugh. "I'm gonna go to bed. I'm not getting' in the middle of this parental crisis."

Cordite hopped onto the couch and curled up next to PC. She absently rubbed his ears, then glanced at Rose. *Well, it's not like she's going to turn up pregnant.*

Rose adjusted her red pillbox hat as PC hung the blue hand-icapped tag on the rear-view mirror. Before she could get out to assist her mother, Terry had sprung out of the car, opened Rose's door, and taken her hand to steady her. With a little bow, he presented her cane. *Looking pretty spry for an old guy.*

He certainly had his own sense of style, starting with a tan derby hat. He'd tucked a reddish pink rose in the hatband. A crisp white dress shirt was the canvas for a mustard yellow sport coat buttoned over a navy vest, all accented by a vibrant red tie. He looked like he'd stepped out of a children's book about an eccentric old gentleman.

Justice came around the front of the car and rolled her eyes at Rose and Terry, grinning and holding hands. "Get a room," she muttered, *almost* under her breath.

Rose wore a periwinkle lace dress with a mother-of-the-bride vibe. Justice dressed up her usual jeans with a violet silk shirt and a red garden party hat. PC, having brought nothing but polo shirts and khaki slacks, topped her tan pants with a navy shirt.

As they made their way up the path to the house, PC gaped at the restored Victorian. She remembered it as a decrepit eyesore, with peeling, faded paint. But now, it was a delicate pink with crisp white trim that looked like lace. Dove grey shingles covered the roof, and the heavily pruned roses by the front were already re-sprouting. Two peacocks and a bevy of peahens combed through the bright green winter ryegrass lawn.

Terry helped Rose up to the five steps onto the wrap-around veranda.

A young woman in a green Victorian dress opened the door. "Welcome!" She gestured for them to enter.

The inside was even more Victorian than the outside. Brunch was being served in a large dining room, which was extended by an equally large conservatory, straight ahead. Female waitstaff wore long skirts and bustles. Males wore brown and tan striped waistcoats. It was like stepping into a time machine.

PC trailed behind as the hostess led her party to a table. She was so busy looking at the immaculate restoration that she bumped into Drew and nearly knocked him over.

"I am so sorry." She felt her cheeks redden. "Are you okay?"

"Of course! I'm fine. You didn't hurt my throwing arm." He smiled as he rubbed his shoulder.

"Drew! Oh, my goodness. So good to see you," Rose gushed. "You're not eating alone, are you? Primrose, please go and keep Drew company. I insist! We'll be fine." She looked at Terry and giggled.

Justice rolled her eyes.

"Ooooh!" A diner with a plate full of seafood passed by, and Rose studied it. "Poor Imogene! Too bad she had to work this morning. She sure does love those oysters."

"Mama, I—"

"Go." She waved PC away.

PC's jaw clenched, but she forced a smile.

"Daisy!" Rose raised her hand high and waved at PC's sister.

Daisy raised her mimosa. The two beefy young men who sat on the other side of the table nearly obscured her. One of them was Tyson, her son. PC didn't recognize the other. It was definitely not Tyson's brother, Zachary.

"So, where are we sitting?" She would have sat with Drew anyway, given that they'd already discussed it, but her mother's insistence rankled. She was not a child to be commanded to the kids' table.

"Over there by the window. You want to grab a plate before we head over?"

"Sure."

As PC stood in the omelet line, she scanned the room. Once a detective, always a detective. She noticed a man in a white shirt and blue tie sitting alone, messing with his phone. A fresh plate of food steamed in front of him. A glass of water, half a glass of orange juice, and a mug of coffee stood guard around his meal. Although he didn't appear to be sad at attending a romantic Valentines' brunch alone, it felt off to her, but she didn't know why. Her eyes continued to survey her surroundings.

Worse than being single at a romantic brunch, a couple was arguing through gritted teeth, trying to keep their voices down. She stabbed at her strawberries as if they needed killing. He poured far too much sugar into his coffee. PC had to look away from that train wreck.

She saw some familiar faces. Woody–Chief Wilson–and his mother were in the dessert buffet line. She recognized some other officers at adjacent tables. Hiro Tran, the young officer who'd helped her free Rocky, was there with his girlfriend, Annie. *What is that? Cop Corner?*

"Next!"

"Um…" PC stammered at the apron-adorned man in front of her.

"What would you like in your omelet?"

She eyed the bewildering array of omelet fillings: bacon, sausage, three kinds of mushrooms, shrimp, several varieties of cheese, a few things she couldn't quite identify–*is that kimchi?* –and an assortment of vegetables. PC gave up halfway through looking at bins because the line was getting long behind her. "Asparagus… portabella mushrooms… that cheese." She pointed to a container of white shreds.

The detective continued to survey the room for familiar faces. She noticed Quan and Lin Youn, her mother's next-door neighbors. They were also Annie's parents.

"Here you go, ma'am. Next!"

The plate was heavier than PC expected. It drooped, and she quickly righted it before the eggs slid onto the floor.

She almost dropped them again, gawking as Hiro Tran got down on one knee and opened what was unmistakably a jewelry box for Annie. The young woman covered her mouth with her hands and started crying, just nodding her head. Hiro slipped the sparkling ring on her finger.

All of Possumwood PD seemed to be there, and they stood up, clapping. PC awkwardly tried to clap with her plate in her hand but ended up just slapping her thigh instead. Woody started toward the happy couple. *I'll congratulate them later.*

"Happens every year." Drew said when she sat down at their table.

"Hiro and Annie get engaged?"

"Nooo. At least one couple gets engaged. One year, it was four."

Romance floated in the air like a fluffy pink cloud, and PC squirmed in her chair. "Well, that's... very nice." She dug into her omelet.

She was three bites into it when the man who had been quietly arguing with his wife stood up and ran toward the restrooms. He got about halfway there when he fell to his knees, moaning and scratching at his face.

Chapter 2

"DREW! CALL 911!"

He hesitated.

"Now!"

He fumbled his phone out of his pocket and started dialing. PC ran over to the man on the floor. He panted and clawed at his mouth.

"Burns! Burns!" he gurgled.

She thought he might be choking and worked to move him into position for the Heimlich maneuver, but his body just went limp whenever she pushed or pulled–it would have been easier to nail Jell-O to a tree. His panting changed to gasping.

PC was vaguely aware of a shadow falling across her as she loosened the man's tie and unbuttoned his collar, but neither of those things helped.

"That's my husband!"

Possumwood's finest rushed to help. Hiro rotated the man's head back to open his airway.

"Ca breef," the man rasped. His fingers dug at his throat.

PC was focusing on him, but she heard someone behind her say, "It's okay, Janelle. It's going to be okay. They're doing everything they can."

PC gave her head a tiny shake. *You should never make promises you can't keep. Where are those paramedics?*

The man's face and throat were not swollen, or else she would have given him an emergency tracheotomy–she'd done it once before, and her patient had survived.

"Move! Move! Move!" came from over her shoulder. The gurney clattered over the threshold.

"What happened?" shouted a middle-aged woman with a 'Possumwood Volunteer EMS' baseball cap on her head.

PC stood. "He got up and started running toward the bathrooms, then fell. He says he's having trouble breathing, and he was scratching at his face and neck, saying it burned."

A second EMT started taking vitals. "Belle! Get the oxygen."

There was a thump behind PC, and she turned to see Woody dropping to the floor. An officer failed to catch him. China clattered as several diners attempted to get up, then fell. Her eyes snapped to Rose's table, but she and her friends were unaffected. She didn't see Daisy and her entourage, but they'd been further away, and there was a horde of people milling about now.

Then she noticed Drew's chair was empty.

Where was he?

PC hurried in the direction of their table, then saw him sprawled on the floor.

"Drew!" She rolled him over onto his back.

His mouth twitched, and he tried to rub his face, but his uncoordinated efforts alarmed PC. "What's going on?"

"Legs... don't... work. Lips... burn. Feel... all... floaty."

14

"Breathing okay?"

"Yuh." His eyelashes fluttered.

"Stay with me. You're going to be fine." *Now who was making sketchy promises?*

Behind her, police that weren't helping with stricken diners were evacuating the unafflicted. Radios crackled and more EMTs were requested.

Drew coughed.

What if he vomits? "Can you sit up?"

She tried to help him, but he was boneless. PC rolled him onto his side and propped his head on his arm in the recovery position. She adjusted the bend of his knee to make sure he didn't fall into a prone position.

"There's another one over here!" Hiro's voice was right behind her.

Belle kneeled and took Drew's vitals, then wrote something on a piece of tape and stuck it on his bicep.

"What's happening?" PC asked.

"Food poisoning? Not sure. We're trying to get more ambulances."

And then she was gone.

Dr. Priyanka Chowdry, who ran the clinic in town, arrived with her nurse. So far, four people had collapsed.

Hiro returned to where PC waited with Drew. "There's a call out to nearby towns for ambulances. Some can double up on patients. They tried Hermann Hospital, but Life Flight's already out on a call."

Diners murmured as two officers herded the unaffected out-side. Belle and her partner loaded the original victim and Woody into one ambulance. Within minutes, another arrived and took Drew and another man.

Two other diners lay on the floor. PC's hand flew to her mouth, and she ran to the stricken foodies.

One of them was Daisy. The other was Tyson's friend. They were lying almost head-to-head.

"Daisy? Daisy!" PC kneeled beside her sister.

Daisy groaned and stuck out her tongue, as if she were trying to get rid of a nasty taste. A piece of tape with her vitals was the only evidence that she'd been triaged, except, perhaps, that she, too, was in the recovery position.

PC brushed Daisy's hair off of her cheek. "It's going to be okay. Ambulance is almost here. You're going to be just fine." *I hope.*

She turned to the stocky teen. His symptoms didn't seem as severe as the others. He was conscious, and able to speak a little.

"What's your name?" PC asked him.

"Sam."

"Okay, Sam. Help is on the way. Try to relax."

PC looked at her FlitBit. It had been almost fifteen minutes since the second ambulance departed.

"There's another EMS squad that's almost here," Tran's voice startled her–she hadn't heard him coming up behind her.

"The bad news," he continued, "is that it can only transport one patient, and the next closest one is forty minutes out."

PC looked from her sister to the teenager. "I have to go in with Daisy and Tyson. Sam here doesn't seem as bad as the others. I can take him in my car."

Tran shook his head. "What if he crashes on you?"

"He'll be that much closer to the hospital than if he waits for the ambulance that's almost an hour away."

EMTs burst through the door and rolled a stretcher toward the victims. They put Daisy on the gurney, took vitals, and started an IV.

"What hospital?" PC demanded.

One EMT frowned at her.

"I'm her sister. I was told you can't transport more than one—I'll bring Sam," she tilted her head toward to young man, "with me. I need to know what ER to meet you in."

"Not usually how we do things, but… I'll let you know when dispatch gives us an open ER bay. It'll be in Houston. The closest regional hospital isn't any closer and isn't as well equipped."

PC got Tyson to help get Sam to his feet and into her car. He sat in the back with his friend. As she was tucking in Rose's cane into the backseat floorboard, the paramedic shouted the name of the hospital. PC gave him a thumbs-up to show she'd gotten the message.

There was a narrow window in the waiting area. PC stared out of it into the dark, looking at, but not really seeing, traffic flowing down the well-lit freeway below. It had been almost two hours since they'd arrived at the emergency room, but she was too restless to sit down. She was too distressed to feel her usual anxiety at being in a hospital. *Daisy had to be okay. She just had to. And Drew.*

17

And… Woody. She didn't allow herself to think about any other outcomes. PC had been able to distract herself for a few minutes by drawing a sketch of the dining disaster.

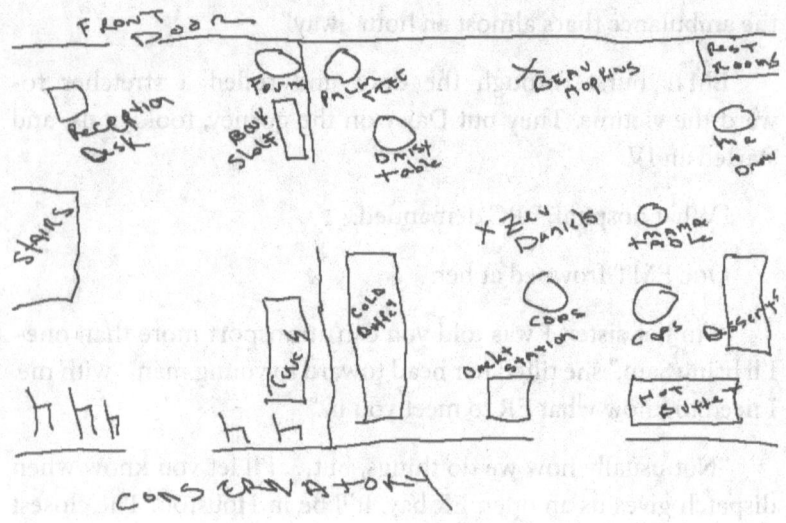

Fortunately, Sunday lunch is a pretty slack time for the ER at Parker Memorial Hospital in west Houston, and all seven patients arrived there. Unfortunately, the first man who showed symptoms arrived DOA, and the man who'd been transported with Drew died shortly after arrival.

An ER doctor came out to speak to the waiting families. Because they didn't know if what was affecting the victims was contagious, the patient area in the ER had been quarantined and the staff had put on biohazard suits. The doc was in regular scrubs, though.

"One of the EMTs noticed fried oysters on the table of one victim. We ran some blood tests and found saxitoxin. We've asked the county health department to test the oysters to confirm, but our diagnosis is paralytic shellfish poisoning. There is no antidote, but with medical support, it should resolve. It will take some time, though. You're free to come back and see your loved ones. I'll come by to talk with you individually."

Nurses directed families to rooms. PC helped Rose to find Daisy. On the way, she noticed no one was looking for Drew. She helped her mother settle in next to Daisy's bed.

Daisy was awake, but groggy. An oxygen mask kept her from speaking.

PC patted her sister's hand. "You just rest. Everything will be all right."

Daisy nodded.

"Mama? I'm going to go check in on Drew."

What little color was left drained from Rose's face. "Drew? He's here?"

PC squeezed her shoulder and walked across the hall. The door was partially open, so she peeked in to check for visitors. Drew was alone. The detective slipped into the room and moved to his bedside. She touched his hand, and his eyelashes fluttered.

"Hey there. How you feeling?" *Stupid question.*

The doctor knocked on the door as he pushed it open. "Are you," he looked at the chart. "Mrs. Berlusconi?"

Say yes. "I'm just a friend."

"Oh." His eyes strayed to Drew. "I can't really discuss his case with you. Do you know if his family is coming?"

"He's got grown kids, but I don't know…"

"Alright. Our staff will try to reach them. In the meantime, I need to evaluate my patient."

The doctor held the door open so PC could leave.

"I'll come back to see you in a little bit," she said, as much to the doctor as to Drew.

By the time she got back across the corridor, Daisy's ex-husband, George, had arrived with the older of their two teenage sons, Zachary. PC couldn't stand George, but at least he was here for the mother of his boys.

He looked at PC as she came in. "You got room for all them in yer car?"

She assumed he meant Rose, Zachary, and Tyson. "Yes."

"Allllright. I gotta get home. TammyJo's havin' a hissy fit 'cause we left off in the middle of buildin' the fahr pit. She'll have my hide if I don't get it done s'afternoon."

PC watched the door close behind him. *Some people bring joy wherever they go. Others, whenever they go.* She shook her head. No two people were more deserving of each other than George and TammyJo, that was for sure.

While Rose chit-chatted with her grandsons, PC grew restless. First, she tried researching 'paralytic shellfish poisoning' on her phone, but the signal was terrible. She wanted to look in on Drew. But she also had to know how Woody was doing. He was an indelible part of her history, even if he had dumped her two days before the homecoming dance in junior year. She slipped out into the corridor, reading names on the doors. When she got to *Wilson, Elwood*, she hesitated. Then she took a deep breath, squared her shoulders, and stepped inside.

Chapter 3

HALF OF THE Possumwood PD seemed to be crammed into Woody's small ER treatment room. Woody's mother, Hilda, sat next to his bed. Hiro and Annie were there, near the door.

It looked bad. Woody was unconscious and hooked up to a ventilator.

PC whispered in Annie's ear. "How is he?"

"Stable, but serious. Doc said it may take a few days for him to breathe on his own. But there's a good chance he'll be okay." Annie sniffled and looked at the floor.

PC wanted to hug her, but she only nodded thoughtfully.

Hiro leaned over behind Annie. "You should go talk to him, PC."

"He's not going to know I was here."

The young officer shook his head. "The nurse told us that they can hear everything anyone says around them. Sometimes they remember, sometimes they don't."

There was something in his eyes. Pleading, maybe? "Alright. I'll go say hello."

She had to worm her way through the officers, some in uniform, some in street clothes, to get to Woody's side. Corrugated blue tubes sprouted from his face and snaked their way back to a machine next to all the other machines by his bed. Cold dread gripped her insides, and she felt exceedingly small and pointless beside the equipment, tubes, and screens.

"Hey, Chief." She took his hand, careful not to dislodge the finger blood pressure monitor. "It's… been a long time. I hope." PC sighed. "I hope you're back on your feet real soon, Woody."

She wasn't sure if she imagined it, or if he really did give her fingers the faintest of squeezes. PC released his hand, gave it a pat, then shuffled out of the room. She mostly felt numb. But fear swirled just beneath the surface, little tendrils of it rising to trace icy paths in her belly.

Yes. Daisy, Drew, and Woody would *probably* make a full recovery. Tyson said that Sam told him he'd be kept overnight for observation and could most likely go home in the morning. There's a lot to be said for being young, strong, and healthy.

Drew's door was ajar. A nurse was in there, changing out his IV fluids. No one had shown up to see him. At least not yet. She thought he'd said his adult kids lived in different states, but she couldn't remember where. Why hadn't she paid more attention when he was telling her about his life? PC mentally kicked herself, then went down the hall to get some water. She didn't know if the nurse was going to do anything more… personal than change the IV, so she waited until the woman left Drew's room.

The detective sipped chilled water from a paper cup near the nurse's station. Two people wearing scrubs were chatting at the desk. The female sat behind the desk, and the male was doing something with paperwork spread out on the Formica counter.

The woman closed a file folder and put it in a black bin. "And this is why I don't eat seafood. That poor guy was just having Valentines' lunch with his wife, now he's dead."

The man glanced around and leaned in, lowering his voice. "Smithers told me that the second one, not the DOA, was in the Mob."

PC held her breath so she could hear what he said.

"Shut the front door!" the woman whispered loudly. "The mafia?"

"That's what she told me. But I haven't seen any FBI agents or anything around."

There was a first time for anything, PC supposed, but she'd never heard of a mob hit involving tainted oysters. They tended to be much more direct. Most likely an unlucky coincidence, if it was even true. How reliable of a source was this Smithers woman, anyway?

Drew's door opened, and the nurse wheeled her cart out into the hallway. As soon as she entered the next room, PC went to visit her friend.

Being semi-conscious and with only an oxygen mask instead of a ventilator, Drew was in better shape than Woody. But not in great shape.

PC stood next to his bed. "Hey, Drew."

His head moved, and he made a noise.

"Don't try to talk."

There was a knock on the doorframe. PC turned to see a woman with tortoiseshell eyeglasses and a long blue cardigan, buttoned only at the top.

"Good afternoon! I'm Maureen, from Admitting. We're getting these poisoning patients moved upstairs. Are you his wife?"

"No."

"I see. Well, somebody'll be in to move him soon."

Maureen left.

PC looked back at Drew. "How about thumbs-up for yes, down for no? How are you feeling?"

He raised his hand slightly off the bed, palm flat, and rotated it slightly from side to side.

"So, medium then?"

He gave her a thumbs up.

"Good," she said out loud. *You're in better shape than some of the others.*

"Is your family coming to be with you?"

Thumbs up.

"Good. I was worried about you being here all alone."

He pointed to her and gave a thumbs-up.

Two men in scrubs came into the room. "Mr. Berlusconi, we're going to move you upstairs, now."

PC patted Drew's hand. "I'd better go check on Daisy. I'll come back later, when you're settled."

Her sister was on a gurney in the hallway when PC came out of Drew's room.

"Primrose!" Rose waved as PC approached. "I'm gonna stay here with Daisy. Could you run the boys home and feed the critters? And send Rocky back with my pills?"

"Sure, Mama." She leaned over awkwardly and kissed Rose on the head. Then she gestured to her nephews. "Come on, guys."

The silence on the way back to Possumwood was uncomfortable. But they didn't want to talk, and PC had no idea what to say to the boys. She knew they were trying to act tough, but they were just kids. Daisy would *probably* be fine, but it was out of PC's hands.

The pale winter sun was just about to kiss the horizon when the Possumwood city limits sign hove into view.

Tyson leaned forward and said, "My truck's at the brunch place."

That was closer than Daisy's house. "Are you guys going to be okay alone? If you don't want to stay at your dad's, I can find a place for you to sleep at your grandmother's."

"It's okay, Aunt P. We gotta be in the weight room early tomorrow before class. We'll be all right," Zach said. "Maybe Mom'll be ready to come home by the time school finishes."

"Is there food at the house? You need groceries?"

"Nah. We're good."

"Thanks, though," Tyson chipped in.

A handful of vehicles dotted the parking lot of Happily Ever Afters, one of them being Tyson's. PC parked near it, let them out, and then watched as they drove away. Several SUVs clustered near the entry, Mirabella County seal decals on their doors.

A man wearing a jacket emblazoned with the same seal carried a small ice chest out the front. Two young women, a blonde and a brunette, followed him out onto the verandah. PC rolled down her window, just a little, so she could hear what was going on.

"But they've always been a reliable supplier–we've never had any trouble with them," said the dark-haired woman.

The man gestured with the box. "Well, we didn't find any obvious code violations, but we'll get these samples tested so we can find the source of the contamination. I'm sorry, but I'm going to have to suspend your food service permit until we get to the bottom of this."

"But we have guests at the B&B!" The blonde gestured toward the house.

"I hope they like takeout. We'll let you know when we get the lab results."

"Simone." The brunette put her hand on the blonde's shoulder. "It's okay. They'll probably check out, anyway. He's just doing his job."

"We did nothing wrong!"

"I know." She pulled the blonde closer. "And that'll be proven in the investigation."

"Yeah? Well, I hope that happens before all of our March bookings cancel." Simone stormed back inside.

Three other county employees came out of the house as the man locked the ice chest into a compartment in his truck. "Miz Reynolds, I'm real sorry. It's nothing personal."

The brunette gave him a fragment of a smile. "I know."

He took a step closer to her. "I'll check to see if Harris County has any space to expedite this. If we send it out to our regular company, we might get results back next week, or it may be next month. I'll see what I can do for you."

"Thank you. I really appreciate that."

He got in his SUV and drove away, followed by the rest of his team. The brunette watched them go.

PC got out of her car. "Excuse me? Ma'am? Are you one of the owners?"

The woman stiffened, suspicion hardening her features. "Who's asking?"

"I'm PC Donovan. I'm in town, looking after my mom. My sister, Daisy, was hospitalized after... um... brunch."

"I'm very sorry to hear that."

"The ER doctor said they thought it was shellfish poisoning. Don't know if that helps. They think everybody will recover. Except for the two that died, of course." PC cringed. That didn't come out at all the way she intended.

"Thanks?"

"I'm sorry. I didn't mean—"

"It's okay. The inspector already told us about the shellfish theory. I'm Caitlyn. Caitlyn Reynolds. Would you like some coffee? Simone was making a pot of decaf a few minutes ago."

PC swallowed. *It's not like she's going to put oysters in the coffee.* "Sure." She glanced at her FlitBit. *Poor Cordite. The odds that Rocky has taken him out to pee are between slim and none, and Slim just got outta town. Why did I accept her invite?*

She paused to get a better view of a bubbling fountain near the walkway. "This place is amazing. You've done so much with it. When I was growing up here, it was just the falling-apart mansion that nobody went anywhere near, unless it was kids, trying to scare each other. The Old Brenderman place. Rumor had it that Mr. Brenderman never left." PC quickly shook her head. "I never believed in that stuff, though."

Caitlyn tightened her lips into what may or may not have been a smile. "Come back for our Halloween haunted house tour. You might run into him."

The door creaked open behind them. "Cait, I'm serious. If that Campbell wedding cancels in March, we aren't going to make the mortgage–oh. Hello."

"Simone, this is PC Donovan. PC, this is my wife, Simone."

"Oh. It's nice to meet you both. I just wish…"

"It was under better circumstances?" Caitlyn finished her sentence.

Simone cocked her head at her spouse.

"PC's sister was one of the buffet… victims."

Simone's expression was hard to read in the twilight. "I'm very sorry about your sister."

"Thanks. Can I take a rain check on the coffee? I've got to go feed Mama's menagerie."

Caitlyn tucked a stray lock of hair behind her ear. "Of course."

There were two gates to Happily Ever Afters, one on the north side of the property, and the other on the south. Each gate was topped by a wrought-iron arch of intricate scroll work that was interwoven with blooming pink roses. The gates could be closed and locked, but now, at least, the south gate stood open. She couldn't see the other one to know its status. The detective rolled through the south gate.

PC had to slam on her brakes as a man in filthy jeans and a denim-shirt stepped out in front of her. He half-heartedly held up his palm to her and continued to stand in her way, gesturing at something out of sight. She leaned forward and caught a glimpse of some men standing around a rock that looked like they'd stolen it from Stonehenge. A noise, perhaps a mower, drowned out their conversation. She hadn't rolled the window up since she'd eavesdropped on the health inspector's conversation with Caitlyn Reynolds a few minutes ago.

A forklift trundled up onto the road and wheeled toward a flatbed trailer. After it got up the ramp and the operator killed the engine, the conversation was quite clear.

An older man in a plaid shirt and cardigan patted the standing stone. "Ha! This ought to keep them damn outta-towners off of my lawn. And those peacocks! I'm just waitin' for one of them to come struttin' into my yard. I'll deep fry it with Cajun marinade under its skin."

The guy in the road dropped his arm and moved out of the way. PC drove forward. *Guess not everyone likes Happily Ever Afters.*

After she'd given Rose's car keys and medications to Rocky, PC took her dog out to run in the back yard while she did the barnyard chores.

The detective thought she'd latched the door to the feed room behind her, and that's why she was so startled when she felt a caress, working its way up the back of her leg toward her derriere. She grabbed the closest weapon, a manure fork, and whirled to face her assailant.

Maaaa maaa maa! Hazel scolded her.

"You crazy goat! You almost gave me a heart attack. I'm getting your dinner–keep your hair on."

She shooed Hazel out, but the goat grabbed something off the floor before she hopped outside.

PC ran after her. "Come back with my phone!"

Hazel pogoed triumphantly around the pen, while Arthur and Guinevere brayed for their supper. PC ducked back into the feed room and grabbed the buckets of pellets she'd been measuring out.

"Hazel! Dinner!" She shook the bucket.

The goat dropped the phone and sprang over to her feeding station. PC doled the food into the bins and hurried to retrieve her device. It wasn't too hard to locate. The screen was lit up, and Hazel had somehow navigated to an obscure shopping channel.

Well, at least she didn't have a credit card number to buy, for the low, low price of $39.99, the one gross of purple plastic stretchy spiders that she'd put in the cart.

Chapter 4

CORDITE WHINED AT PC from the floor. She yawned and glanced at her FlitBit.

"You couldn't have waited twelve minutes for the alarm to go off?"

The dog whined again.

"Fine."

PC got out of bed and threw on some critter-feeding clothes. Cordite trotted around the yard, re-marking his territory, while PC fed the three and four-leggeds, then released the hens from their coop. She made a point of leaving her phone inside, just in case Hazel had another bout of retail fever.

Her thoughts wandered to Daisy, Drew, and Woody as she did the scooping up after the animals. She put the manure and shavings in a pile near the gate. Rose's friend, Justice, showed up to retrieve it for her mushroom farming operation every three or four days.

How had Rose fared during the night? Sleeping in one of those hospital chair things isn't all that comfortable, but she knew her mother wouldn't leave Daisy's side. She'd better pack some fresh clothes for Rose and make sure she got her walking done and breakfast eaten. PC hadn't taken her evening run last night, and this morning, she felt restless and itchy. She could probably fit in a quick jog before she left for the hospital–she had to take a shower, anyway.

"C'mon, Cordite!"

The dog shivered. It had been cold enough last night to frost the roof–but not the grass–and, if it were visible behind the curdled clouds, the sun would only just now be floating over the edge of the world,.

The screen door of the porch snapped shut behind them, and as soon as they were back in the house, Cordite burrowed under an afghan on the couch.

"Lightweight. I guess I won't be taking you with me after all."

She changed shoes and scooped her keys into her pocket. Rose's keys were not on the end table. *Where was Rocky? Had he fallen off the wagon? Been in a wreck? Skipped town?*

She forced herself to take a deep breath. *Call Rocky first, before you jump to conclusions.*

PC called her brother. Three rings, then "You have reached the voice mailbox—"

She disconnected. *That doesn't mean he's flown the coop. Or had an accident.* She tried convincing herself, without much luck. *Ever since Daddy died, Rocky had a terrible time sticking with anything. If he couldn't stay with Darla and their kid, a custodian job at the nursing home wasn't going to hold him long.* PC sighed and turned to the afghan that covered Cordite. "Never mind the run. I'm getting in the shower."

She was still drying off when her phone rang.

"Rocky? Where are you?"

"Well, good mornin' to you, too. I was drivin' when you called earlier. Miss Durelle wanted me to pick up some supplies for the Manor, seein' as I had Mama's car. Didn't think she'd be needin' it today, so I came out to get this stuff. It's kinda between Conroe and the airport."

"When I saw the keys were missing, I was worried—"

"That I stole Mama's car and run off?"

"That you were dead in a ditch somewhere." PC blotted her hair. "I just got out of the shower, and I'm about to go to the hospital."

"Ew! Are you talkin' on the phone to me nekkid?"

"Bye, Rocky."

PC knocked as she entered Daisy's room. Rose was in the corner chair, head leaned against the wall. Her skin was grayish. She could only see Daisy's feet, and she held her breath as she came into the room.

"Oh, PC! Come on in!" Daisy called out to her.

Her sister was sitting up in bed with the TV on and a People Magazine in her lap. The full oxygen mask had been replaced by tubing that clipped to her nose.

"What a difference a day makes. You look great! How do you feel?"

"Still cain't keep nothin' down, but at least I can breathe right. Probably go home tomorrow."

PC sat in the chair by Daisy's bed. "You already called the boys? Need me to check on them?"

"No, no. They're comin' up after school."

"Good." PC nodded. "How 'bout you, Mama? You don't look like you slept."

Rose waved her hand dismissively. "I'm fine."

"Have you had any breakfast?"

"Yeah. They brought some up. Kinda like room service at a hotel."

The door swung open, and in walked a woman that PC guess-timated was somewhere between retirement age and elderly.

She shook a battered manila envelope. "I told you. I told you, Rose Donovan. Now you've almost lost your baby girl, maybe you'll finally believe me, and sign my petition."

"Petition? Mabel, what are you talking about?" Rose barely moved in her seat.

"The petition I made to shut down that tourist magnet bed-and-breakfast wedding place. My nephew, Beau Hopkins, would not be in the coroner's office right now if it wasn't for those outsiders. They don't belong here and need to go back where they come from."

"Miz Radcliffe," Daisy sat as straight as she could amongst her lines and tubes. "I beg to differ. They bring in a lot of business to this town. A lot. Probably a third of the customers at Karla's Kurls are ladies wantin' their hair fixed up for the fancy goings on at the Afters. Miss Caitlyn and Miss Simone, they've been real good about sending clients our way."

"That's just what I mean!" Mabel shook her envelope again. "The outsiders just attract more outsiders. They don't have people here; they don't care about people here! They don't have roots. It's all about filthy lucre!" Mabel spat.

"Humph. I like havin' that extra filthy lucre in my check. Most of those ladies tip real good. Unless you're volunteerin', now, to help out with my mortgage, you can take your petition and—"

"Daisy! It's alright. Just relax. She's upset about her nephew." The heart rate monitor's surge in spikes alarmed PC. "Ms. Radcliffe, you have our deepest condolences."

Rose sat up. "Mabel, how did you even get here? I know you don't drive anymore."

Mabel thrust out her chin. "I rode with Janelle. She had to sign some papers or something. She is such a rock. So unruffled, so strong."

"I see. Let me see your petition, hon."

Daisy fumed as Mabel smugly handed over the envelope.

Rose pulled out the contents. "How many signatures you reckon you need?"

"Um... I don't know. But plenty of people will sign. I'm sure of it."

Rose looked down at the paper again before tucking it back into the envelope. "Mabel. Honey, you've only got one signature on here, and it's yours."

Mabel's nostrils flared, and her cheeks burned. She snatched the petition before turning on her heel and storming out of the room.

Daisy chuckled.

Mabel's voice screeched in the hallway. *Was she harassing Drew?*

"I'm just going to see what's happening." PC gave Daisy's hand a squeeze before she got up.

In the corridor, hospital security was trying to escort Mabel Radcliffe out of the building, but she was having none of it.

"I have every right to be here! Unhand me!"

A Possumwood PD officer came out of Woody's room and spoke to her quietly. After a few minutes, she took his arm, and they headed toward the elevators.

PC wanted to see if the old harpy had been bothering Drew, so she stalked to his door. She knocked before she opened it, and she thought she heard someone say, "Come in!"

So, she did.

But Drew was not alone.

There were three adults who appeared to be in their mid-twenties, two males and one female, standing at the back of the room. Next to his bed, a slender, elegant woman with shiny black hair pulled up in a French twist sat talking to him. The standing woman looked like her mini-me. Actually, she looked like her younger sister.

"Oh." PC blurted. "I didn't realize…"

Drew was also down to just some oxygen tubing. "Come in, come in. This is my son Connor, my daughter Aisling, and her husband Troy. And their mother, Fiona. This is my… friend, PC—"

"It's nice to meet you all. You're busy. I'll catch up with you later." PC backed out of the door before Drew could say anything.

She went across the hall to Woody's room. PC expected it would be full of cops, so she didn't stand on ceremony–just walked right in. Woody, unfortunately, had not had the near-miraculous recovery that Daisy and Drew had. He was still on the ventilator.

She squatted next to Annie Youn, the only PPD personnel in the room. Hilda was reading a book by his bed. PC supposed the entire Possumwood Police force couldn't hang out in Woody's Houston hospital room forever. "How's he doing?"

"About the same. No better, but no worse, either."

The Woody Wilson she remembered from forty years ago was strong as an ox, and just as bull-headed, truth be told. It wasn't right, him lying there completely helpless. When the landmarks suddenly change, sometimes it's hard to figure out where you are in the world. PC was too uncomfortable to stay long.

Hilda looked up from her book, her face drawn, and smiled softly at PC.

The detective touched Woody's hand. "Hey, Chief. I just came by to check on you. You're going to be back on your feet before you know it."

PC wasn't sure that was true, but she wasn't about to let on otherwise.

Chapter 5

PC PULLED INTO Rose's driveway and opened the car door.

"No, Renetta, Capra Leche Farm is not for sale! The Marbergers already own half the town–they don't need my land, too."

Rose and PC looked at each other.

"That sounds like Justice." Rose fumbled with the door handle.

PC jumped out and ran around to grab her mother's cane from the back seat before she got out of the car and fell. Last thing they needed was for her to break the other hip.

They hurried around the side of the house to see the local real estate agent, Renetta Sherman, leaning against the fence. Justice was inside the pen, scooping donkey donuts and goat grapes into a burlap bag. Guinevere supervised while Arthur and Hazel nibbled hay near the barn.

"They're offering twice what it's worth."

"Maybe what it's worth to you. It's my place and I'm not sellin'. Why don't you go bother them gals down at the weddin' chapel? They may need the money after the Health Department gets through with 'em."

Rose coughed. "Afternoon, Renetta."

"My stars! I haven't seen you in ages, Rose. How'd that surgery go? You're lookin' good."

"Thank you. Now what's all this about you trying to buy Justice out?"

"Not me! No, no. Thorne Marberger was interested in—"

Rose's eyebrow arched. "This wouldn't have anything to do with that new section of the tollway that's supposed to open up in the fall does it?"

"Um, well, I, um, wouldn't know anything about that. My client's looking on the east side of town to—"

"Put in a dollar store strip center? Apartments? That toll road will probably cut twenty minutes or more off the drive into Houston. And if they ever get around to doin' that high-speed rail, well how far are we from that proposed station?"

Renetta drew herself up and pursed her lips. "There is nothing illegal, or immoral, about making a profit in real estate."

Rose crossed her arms. "Land speculation has always been popular with the robber baron class."

"You're just jealous, Rose Donovan, that Thorne has money to invest in large-scale projects."

"No one loves Thorne Marberger more than Thorne Marberger. I feel bad for anyone who has to put up with his nonsense."

Renetta flicked her wrist so that she could glance at her watch, and the sapphire pavé bezel sparkled, even in the dull sun of a late winter afternoon. "I have another appointment. If you'll excuse me."

She slipped into her decade-old Mercedes and sped away.

"And good riddance!" Justice called after the departing car.

"Don't be so hard on her. Renetta's not a bad person, not really." Rose sighed. "Real estate business has got to be tough out here in the sticks. Cozying up to Thorne Marberger is probably a good idea, if you're looking for a client with a lot of money to spend."

Justice crossed her arms. "His daddy, Preston, must be spinning in his grave. He'd never pressure anybody to sell their family farm."

"I'm partial to Cort, myself. He treats Lily like a princess."

Justice swung the bag of dung up into the bed of the truck and grinned. "I'd forgot your sister married into the Marberger clan. I guess if Thorne was my kin, I'd move to Vermont, too."

Rose chuckled. "Come in for a hot drink?"

Justice looked down at her clothes. "Thanks, but I'll skip it. Next time, when I'm more presentable. Gotta turn this into the compost pile before it gets too dark. Has to be well-rotted for the mushrooms."

PC made a face. That was way more information than she wanted about mushroom farming. She waved to Justice as the wiry woman climbed into the cab of her truck, then turned to her mother. "Let's get you inside. You must be exhausted."

Rose didn't argue, and PC held all the doors open for her so she could go plop down in her recliner. Humming while she plugged in the electric kettle, she got out mugs and tea bags.

"Mama? What kind of tea you want?"

There was no reply.

PC poked her head into the living room, and saw that Rose was fast asleep. She was unfolding an afghan to cover her mother when Rocky came in. PC raised a finger to her lips, and he nodded. After she draped the blanket over Rose, her brother followed her into the kitchen. The kettle was boiling by then, and she made them each a cup of tea.

"How's Daisy? Must be better if Mama's come home."

"She'll probably be released tomorrow."

"That's cool. Too bad they didn't let her go today."

"Yeah, I called Zach on the way home. He and Tyson were going to get dinner at the Brisk Rib. I'm sure they'll be glad to have their mama home, but I think they're liking going out to eat. I expect it makes them feel grown up."

Rose began to snore. The kind of snore that frightens pets and small children.

Rocky snickered. "Yeah. Hey, do you know what's goin' on at the weddin' place? There was at least three cop cars out there, lights flashing, when I was coming home."

Cordite trotted in from the living room and flopped under the table at PC's feet.

"Really? I hadn't heard anything."

She got out her phone and texted Hiro. The reply came back almost immediately.

"Someone threw a brick wrapped in a note through the front door glass, telling them to get out or else. Reviewing security footage."

Chapter 6

"WHAT?" ROCKY ALMOST spilled his tea.

"That's crazy." PC shook her head. She understood people were upset by the shellfish poisoning fiasco, but it was an accident. It wasn't even their fault. *Hope it doesn't cost them their business. Or their lives.*

Cordite jumped up and ran out of the kitchen, barking. There was a knock at the front door. Rocky and PC looked at each other, as if drawing straws to see who had to answer it. They both got up, though, and went through the living room to find the dog leaping up to eyeball someone through the glass window as he made little yipping sounds.

Annie waved hesitantly as PC approached. She opened the door.

"I'm sorry to bother you. My parents are both at the store, and my car won't start. Is there any way you could possibly run me to the station?"

"Of course. Come on in. I'll get my shoes on."

"Hey, Annie." Rocky returned to the kitchen.

She leaned over to pet Cordite, and he jumped up, trying to lick her face, nearly ramming his nose into her eye.

"Sorry about that. Five years, and I've never been able to break him of that." She shrugged on her jacket and grabbed her car keys. "Ready?"

The dog insisted on going, and PC didn't have a good reason for him to stay, so she grabbed the leash from beside the door and snapped it on his collar. "C'mon, you little tyrant."

"Thanks, again. Usually, I'd call Hiro, but he's in the middle of investigating the Afters incident."

"I heard about that. Crazy, huh?"

Annie slid into the car. Cordite popped into the back seat on PC's side and stood on the floor with his front feet on the console between the driver and passenger seats.

"It's worse than you think. The guy from Houston that died? His name was Zev Daniels. Apparently, he was going to testify before a grand jury, about his former company Noren Corp., using some highly creative accounting."

"That *does* seem like an awfully strange coincidence." PC started backing out of the driveway. *And there are very few genuine coincidences in this world.*

"It was all hush-hush until he turned up dead. Now every outlet is covering it. Don't you read the news?"

"I've been at the hospital with Daisy or looking after Mama all day. By the way, any updates on Woody, uh, Chief Wilson?"

"No. He's about the same."

"Well, I hope he comes out of this soon."

"We all do."

A stiff silence filled the car. Cordite yapped at the occasional pedestrian, but mostly dropped fur onto the upholstery. It took less than ten minutes to make it to downtown Possumwood. PC pulled up into the PPD parking lot.

"Thank you so much. I really appreciate the ride."

"Any time."

PC watched the young woman disappear into the building before she backed out of the parking space. On the way home, the detective made a point of going out of her way to drive past Happily Ever Afters (no more cruisers) and Drew's gallery. She wasn't sure if she felt more relieved or sad that the lights were out. At least no one was inside sifting through his belongings.

It had been a shock to see his straight-out-of-a-Ralph-Lauren-advertisement family. She almost felt like she was the secret side piece who suddenly discovers that she's the secret side piece, when she thought she was the main squeeze. But that was ridiculous. She and Drew didn't have a romantic relationship. And he and his wife had been divorced for years. PC was irritated with herself that she didn't hang around at least a couple of minutes to talk to Drew. But she had felt like a fifth wheel, and her sense of not belonging was acute. She was used to being in charge of the situation, and this hapless feeling was more than uncomfortable. So, she left. Like she always did. She could stand over the ripest, most putrescent corpse without a twinge, but being around people with an undercurrent of hostility? She'd flee every time she could.

She was fairly sure she knew why, though. This idea, this thought, had wormed its way through her brain, gnawing at her reason for so many years. If only the last conversation she'd had with Mike hadn't been a fight. It was so stupid. Catering menu for the wedding. Did it really matter what the mushrooms were stuffed with? Probably, it was pre-wedding jitters. But she always wondered if Mike was getting cold feet. Had this pointless bickering distracted him when he needed to focus? Was it her fault he was dead?

Cordite whined.

"What? Now you have to pee? Cross your legs - we'll be home soon."

Everyone else was asleep, even though it was only 10:30. But PC changed position in her bed for the fourth time in the past five minutes. Cordite seemed almost annoyed enough to jump off onto the floor. The detective was trying to read a mystery novel she'd found lying on her mother's coffee table, but she struggled to focus on it. Partly because the writer's research was terrible, and they failed to get procedure right most of the time, and partly because she couldn't get the brick out of her head.

Who was threatening Simone and Caitlyn? They hadn't *intended* to kill anyone. It hardly seemed fair to hold them accountable for their supplier's mistake. But then again, her sister was going to be just fine. She wondered if some attorney somewhere was already gearing up for a class action lawsuit.

PC looked at her watch again. 10:32. She texted Tran. "Any luck with surveillance vid?"

It was a full fifteen minutes before he replied. "No. Baggy clothes, hoodie and a baseball cap, gloves. Can't even determine M/F."

"That sux. Latent prints on note?"

"Still cooking"

"Shout if I can help"

"Will do"

That only made her more curious. One possibility was that the brick thrower knew about the security cameras and had dressed accordingly. PC, who usually noticed those things right off the bat, didn't remember seeing them. Another was that some rando just assumed there would be cameras–they're everywhere now. But who would *know*?

A frequent guest?

Electrician who installed them?

An employee, theirs, or security company's?

Caitlyn or Simone?

PC found it awfully hard to believe that the Reynoldses would do anything to call attention to their situation, when it was in their best interest to give people a chance to forget.

The detective pushed a shopping cart down a grocery aisle. She'd been there too many times before, and dread settled into her stomach. Every time, she tried to find the exit, but it didn't seem to exist. A woman came toward her, pushing her own cart, vacant eyes staring past PC. The detective knew her though. Marissa Blackwell, her first solo case. She averted her eyes, but she didn't need to look – the woman's knife wounds were burned into her memory. Around the corner, a young man stacked turnips in a produce bin. Benito Alvarez. Suicide. More came into the store, and PC knew every single one, both by name and mortal wounds.

She awoke, gasping for air. Cordite was licking her face, and she scooped him up and held him close. When her heartrate slowed, she set him back down. His tail thumped on the bed. PC went into the living room to search for the book she'd been reading earlier. She wasn't going back to sleep for a while.

Suddenly, PC's alarm was beeping, and she startled awake. How did that happen? It was like she went from sixty to zero in four seconds flat. She got dressed in the closet with the door shut, because as soon as Guinevere and Arthur saw the light come on in her room, they started braying for their breakfast. She hoped the neighbors appreciated her sacrifice.

The dream, the one she had after she'd fallen asleep reading, was already slipping away like sand through her fingers, but she tried to remember it. It had been raining bricks. Bricks wrapped in notes. They broke windows and dented roofs. One came down the chimney and bounced off the hearth into her room, although there was no fireplace in the waking world. The brick was wrapped in old parchment paper, and her name was written on it. She unwrapped it and read the note. But PC couldn't remember what it said.

Chapter 7

THE ANIMALS HAD their breakfast, and now PC and Rose were stopping at the City Café for theirs, before they picked up Daisy from the hospital. The Café had the best omelets in town, or at least ones available on a daily basis.

Their server was an average looking young woman with dish-water blonde hair who seemed to have wanted to have been any-where else but at work. Her name tag read, 'Sally.' It took so long for her to bring them two glasses of water and a pot of coffee, PC wondered if she'd left and gone home.

When Sally finally dropped off the carafe, the coffee was cold. But she'd already vanished back into the kitchen before they poured any into their mugs. PC was used to drinking coffee at just about any temperature, but Rose was not happy.

After several minutes passed, PC flagged down another server. "Excuse me? I know we're not your table, but the coffee we were served was cold. Could we get some fresh coffee that's hot?"

"I'm so sorry. I'll bring it right out." She took the cold carafe and sped into the kitchen, Rapunzel-length braid swinging behind her. A minute, or perhaps less, passed before she returned with steaming hot coffee.

"Thank you so much!"

She nodded and went back to her assigned tables.

Fifteen minutes later, Sally returned with their breakfast plates.

"Oh, Honey. I'd ordered dry toast. This is slathered in butter. Could you please bring me some without all that?" Rose pushed the plate of toast, melted butter pooling in the middle of the bread and dripping down the sides, toward the edge of the table.

Tsk. "It's toast. Can't you just eat it?" Sally pursed her lips.

"Excuse you?" PC responded.

"Really? Just scrape the butter off."

"What?" PC was stunned.

"You heard me. Scrape the butter off. It's not that hard. You people have been complaining about everything. I'm just trying to—"

"Sally! Could you come over here, please?" Winnie Hargraves, one of PC's dart buddies and the café's co-owner, beckoned from the cash register.

Sally flew like an angry wasp to her employer. "That table is so—"

"You have been warned. Repeatedly. We really wanted to give you a second chance after you lost your job at the Evers, but I really can't have you talking to my customers that way. You can pick up your check on Friday. Please go."

The busy café had grown silent, diners hushing so as not to miss the spectacle. Who needs reality TV when you've got real-life drama with your breakfast?

"But that's not fair!" Sally's eyes blazed. She raised her head, like a snake about to strike. "I'm going to tell Uncle Wilson."

"You do that. Goodbye, Sally."

Her face an alarming shade of purple, Sally tore off her apron and flung it to the floor before stomping back into the kitchen, presumably to gather her belongings.

"Frida, could you pick up her tables, please, hon?" Winnie turned and smiled at a customer approaching with his check.

"Sure thing," answered the server who'd helped them earlier with the coffee. She took the soggy toast away with her.

After the customer tucked his change into his wallet, Winnie scurried over to PC and Rose's table.

"I'm so sorry about that. Unfortunately, that girl is not one to learn a lesson. We only took her on because she's my sister's husband's brother's niece. If she cannot get a hold of her temper," Winnie shook her head sadly, "she's going to have a hard life ahead of her. Now, because you had to put up with all that, I'll comp your food."

"No, no, no." Rose held up her hands. "You don't need to do that."

"I want to."

Another customer with a check reached the register. Winnie waved to him. "I'll be right there, Delbert." She turned to Rose and PC and pointed to the table. "Breakfast is on me this morning."

She hurried back to the register, and Frida arrived in Winnie's wake, a water pitcher and dry toast.

"Oh, honey. Thank you so much."

A terrible crash from the kitchen caused a collective gasp from the diners. From under the saloon door, a small white plate rolled out on its edge and rattled on the tile as it settled into place.

Jim Hargraves, Winnie's husband, could be heard shouting, "What is wrong with you, Sally?"

"You're not going to fire me and get away with it!"

"Get out before I call the cops!"

Another crash. A door slammed. An engine whined and tires screeched.

Rose and PC followed as Winnie pushed through the door to the kitchen.

"Jim, are you okay?"

He stood behind a mound of broken china. Silverware and food were scattered across the floor. A large stock pot lay on its side in a cheesy puddle, the soup of the day dripping down the wall above it.

Rose gasped.

PC recovered quicker than either of her companions. "What happened?"

"I was back here putting bread in the oven when that, that Hell spawn came storming in here and pushed over the bus cart with the dirty dishes. I asked her what she was doing, then she screamed at me and heaved the soup at me."

Winnie pulled her phone out of her pocket. "I'm going to video this and send it to my sister."

Rose inhaled deeply and sighed. "That's such a tragedy."

Jim looked at the debris field. "The dishes?"

Winnie's gaze fell on the door. "Sally?"

"No. That broccoli cheese soup. My favorite. It's obscene to waste it like that."

Jim cracked a smile.

Winnie tried to shoo them out of the kitchen. "Your food's getting cold."

PC surveyed the destruction. "Is there anything we can do to help?"

Jim shook his head. "No. The dishwasher and I will get it cleaned up in time for the lunch rush. Not sure what I'm going to do about the soup, though."

Daisy was still waiting on her discharge paperwork when PC and Rose arrived to pick her up.

"They said Dr. Hamilton had to go help out in the ER. No tellin' when he'll be back." Daisy sighed. She was dressed and ready to leave, sitting up in her bed and flipping through the twelve channels on the hospital TV.

Rose plopped into the chair closest to the bed and turned to PC. "Primrose, can you go get me a soda water?"

"Sure, Mama."

That was just the excuse she needed to check on Drew and Woody. Woody's room was furthest from the waiting area with the vending machines, so she stopped there first.

It surprised her to find him sitting up in bed, talking to a couple of officers.

"Sorry. I didn't mean to interrupt. You look… a whole lot better." She reached for the door handle.

"PC. It's okay. Come on in."

She stood at the foot of his bed. "It's good to see you awake. How do you feel?"

"I've been better. I heard you've been stopping by. Thanks."

"Sure. I'll let you get back to your staff meeting." She gave an indecisive half wave as she practically bolted from the room.

A nurse was pushing Drew out of his room in a wheelchair, his son at his side.

"PC!"

"Look at you! Almost as good as new." She couldn't help but notice the bandages where his IV lines had been pulled.

"Well, I'm getting there. You remember Connor, right?"

"Of course." She smiled at the young man and nodded.

"He's going to be staying with me a few days to make sure I'm back up to full steam."

"That's a good idea. Are you officially discharged?"

"Yeah. My chauffer came to pick me up this morning." He grinned at Connor.

"Daisy said Dr. Hamilton had to go to ER so he couldn't sign any paperwork."

Connor and Drew shared a glance. Then Drew said, "Well, Dr. Figueroa signed mine. He's in Dr. Hamilton's practice, I believe. Perhaps he can sign off on your sister's papers? I can ask—"

"It's fine. I'll ask the nurse."

Remaining silent, Connor seemed to be in a hurry to get his father out of the hospital.

Or maybe away from me.

PC shifted her weight. "We'll have to have a raincheck for brunch."

Drew shuddered. "The company was flawless. The food... not so much. I don't know if I'll ever be able to look a chocolate mousse in the eye again."

"Come on, Dad. Mom's waiting for us downstairs."

The nurse started pushing the chair.

"Your mother is waiting on *you* to drive her to the airport. But we don't want her to be late for check in." He smiled softly at PC. "When food starts seeming like a good idea, I'll give you a call. You are coming to the Saturday workshop, right? Wilma is amazing with acrylics."

"I'll be there."

Connor hurried ahead to push the elevator buttons while PC made her way to the vending machines.

"What took you so long?" Daisy sniped. She was sitting in her own wheelchair. "The nurse brought the discharge stuff right after you left. We've been sitting around waiting—"

"Daisy. Calm down, honey. I know you're anxious to get home and see your boys. Primrose was checking on her friends." She nodded to the young man in scrubs. "And the nurse only finished explaining the discharge handout about two minutes ago."

Daisy glowered as they headed down the corridor. PC willed Rose to walk faster, but knowing she was doing the best she could.

The brick veneer by the elevators reminded PC of the vandalism at the Afters. Was someone trying to take advantage of the unfortunate oyster incident to try and force Caitlyn and Simone out, or was it just some yahoo with nothing better to do? She wanted to text Tran so she could double check his list of brick-throwing suspects. Were any of them friends of Thorne Marberger or Mabel Radcliffe?

Chapter 8

PC SAT AT the kitchen table with a cup of hot tea. She hadn't even picked up her phone when the text chime sounded. It was Tran.

"Have you heard?"

"What?"

"Tests on oysters neg. Not contaminated."

"??? Then how did they get shellfish poisoning?"

The reply was a photo of a page from the Health Department's report. No dinoflagellates were present. The oysters were safe.

Another image. This time it was a document describing saxitoxin as a WMD–weapon of mass destruction–if used as a biological weapon. The CIA was known to use it in suicide devices.

"How does it end up in buffet? Accident or?"

"Dark Web. Bitcoin. You can get anything. No accident."

"Agreed. Maybe brick thrower is poisoner? Have you looked into ex-employee Sally (don't know surname)?"

"Not yet."

"She's a piece of work."

Tran sent a "wow" emoji.

PC let the news sink in. This now looked like a double homicide. Was this an assassination of a grand jury witness? A missed target? Or an attempt to close down the Afters that went horribly wrong? The "who" would be a lot easier to figure out if she knew the "why."

She was well aware she shouldn't meddle in police business, and she was sure that Woody wouldn't take kindly to that, anyway. But it looked like someone may be trying to throw Caitlyn and Simone Reynolds under the bus and drive the Afters out of business.

PC's reason, the one that throbbed at the core of her being, for joining the police force was to give others the justice that her father had never gotten. Trey Donovan was shot in cold blood at their family-owned convenience store forty years ago. There was never even so much as a suspect identified, much less the killer. It had formed something like a black hole at her center—she kept catching murderers, but still it wanted more. It demanded The Murderer. Perhaps solving this original mystery would plug the hole, but she couldn't be certain. There was so little evidence to go on, and most of the people who knew anything about it were dead.

But this Afters case. Two homicides. PC couldn't just leave it alone. She had been *the police* for so many years. A murder drew her like a moth to a bug zapper–and hopefully, she wouldn't get fried. Besides, if Tran didn't want her help, he wouldn't keep giving her information.

She took a sip of her tea.

First scenario: Was Zev Daniels assassinated before he could testify before a grand jury? People from miles around came to the famous, or perhaps now infamous, Valentine's Brunch at the Afters. It would be normal for non-denizens to be there, and no one would notice a stranger at the busy buffet, sprinkling a little bit of death on… what? If it wasn't the oysters, what was it?

Of course, that led to the second scenario: The trap was laid, but the wrong people fell into it. The poisoner had to have a reasonable expectation that the target would eat the spiked food. Did they have a plan to get rid of it as soon as the intended victim took some? Perhaps they didn't care what happened to the other diners. After all, it would seem very strange if only one person got shellfish poisoning and there was a mountain of oysters. Why didn't they poison the oysters if that was their cover story? Did the mark dislike the shellfish?

Third scenario: Someone is trying to drive Caitlyn and Simone out of business. Who would be willing to risk killing innocent bystanders? A disgruntled former employee with anger management issues? A grumpy neighbor who blames traffic in his yard on the Afters? The crazy petition lady, who may not have a firm grip on reality? Someone else?

Fourth scenario: The mystery food honestly became contaminated, and it was nobody's fault. But that seemed the least likely—who was going to have saxitoxin lying around in their kitchen, or be carrying it in their pocket?

She could ask Drew and Daisy what they'd eaten. With any luck, Tyson's friend, Sam, would recall what he had. There had to be a common thread. She could report that to Tran, and she'd leave it to him to investigate whether Woody or either of the decedents had the same dish. It could be weeks before any tox screens came back.

It was almost time to feed the critters. PC texted Drew before she went out to the barn.

"Hope you are better. Do you remember what you ate at the brunch?"

She was slipping on her shoes when her phone rang.

"Hey, Drew."

"The commandant went to the grocery store. I have a few minutes to talk."

"Your son?"

Drew chuckled. "Yes. He's possibly a little over-zealous."

"I'm glad you're feeling better. And you've got a father-son bonding opportunity."

"Right now, it seems more like a bondage opportunity."

His voice was playful.

"He doesn't want to lose you."

"I know. I'm just kidding around. Now what was it you needed to know?"

Cordite came into the kitchen and whined. She leaned over to scratch his ears.

"What did you eat at the buffet?"

"Let me think." He paused. "They had just put out a pan of chocolate mousse. I wanted to make sure I got some because it goes fast. The Afters is locally famous for it. Strawberries, whipped cream on the side. French toast. What's this about?"

"Just trying to help figure out what food was… contaminated."

"Thought they said it was the oysters. Which seems reasonable, except I didn't have any. So why did I get sick?"

"The oysters, actually, were clean."

"Paralytic shellfish poisoning without the shellfish. Sounds like STX."

"What?" PC's eyebrows knitted together.

"STX. Saxitoxin. Haven't you ever heard of Gary Powers?"

"How do you know this, and who is Gary Powers?"

"1960. He was a U2 spy plane pilot shot down over Russia. He had a quarter with a secret trigger that sprung a needle coated in STX as a suicide device. It was in a podcast I listened to a few weeks ago. Or maybe it was on the History Channel. I can't quite remember. Nasty stuff, though. Anyway, that new Robert LaClancé book that was out a couple of weeks ago featured an assassin who coated all of his bullets and knives in the stuff. Neal Dawson had to take him out before he could get to the president and steal the nuclear codes."

PC laughed and Cordite whined again, louder.

"I never would have pegged you as a thriller junkie."

"I'm not sure if that is a compliment or an insult. But I'm glad I can keep you guessing."

Cordite barked, just once.

"Never boring that way. I've got to take Cordie out to pee. Thanks for calling me back."

"Sure thing. Next time the dungeon master is away, I plan on sneaking over to the gallery. Talk to you soon."

The animals were fed, dinner was eaten, and Rocky and Rose were in the living room watching Netflix. PC started to text Daisy but realized her sister would probably not even notice a message. She located the number in her favorites list and tapped the screen.

"Engleman residence."

PC was surprised by both the formal greeting and the male voice answering Daisy's cell. "Tyson?"

"Aunt P?"

"I was wanting to talk to your mom. How's she doing?"

"Good. She's asleep right now, though."

"Of course. Would you tell her to call me when she gets up?"

"Sure."

"Oh. There's one other thing. You wouldn't by any chance happen to remember what Sam had to eat at brunch, do you?"

Her nephew snorted. "Well, I beat him to the chocolate mousse, and got the last of it, so he had to wait on a new batch. He was stuck with strawberries until they brought some more mousse out–he almost threw some at me. He had some other stuff, not sure what. Is it important?"

"It might be. Thanks, you've been a big help, Ty."

Could some of that "other stuff" have been French toast? Or was it strawberries à la Borgia?

Chapter 9

DAISY FINALLY RETURNED PC's call at 9:30 the next morning. There was a lot of background noise, and PC struggled to hear.

"Where are you?"

"I'm on the way to the shop. Sorry, I got the heat on full blast."

"You just got out of the hospital! Do you really need to go to work today?"

"If I don't cut hair, I don't get paid. You have any idea how much two teenage boys eat?"

"Don't you get child support from George?"

Daisy laughed. "Girl, the judge gave him a sweetheart deal, so he didn't pay much, and Zak turned eighteen two months ago."

PC hadn't realized her sister was that close to the financial edge. She had a little money set aside for emergencies. She could — *Stop. Refocus. Daisy would ask if she needed help.*

PC forced herself to switch mental gears. "I know it's going to sound weird, but do you remember what you ate at the brunch?"

"What?"

"The Valentine's brunch. What did you eat?"

"You called to ask me that?"

"Yes."

"Well. I had some strawberries, but they weren't sweet. French toast. Sausage. Green salad. Some potato thing."

"Anything else?"

"Isn't that enough? I have to watch my figure, you know."

"Thanks, Daisy. Have a good day."

PC did some of her best thinking while she was walking, so she decided to take Cordite for a stroll. The sun was out, and it was 54 degrees, according to the thermometer on the side of the barn. Perfect for a ramble.

Whos and whys and hows tumbled over in her mind like clothes in a dryer. PC hadn't been paying much attention to where they were going, mostly following Cordite, and keeping them both out of the street. He veered down an alley and broke her out of her reverie.

"What are you doing, you crazy dog?"

Cordite was tugging her toward the faded yellow skip behind the City Café.

"No. We're not going dumpster diving. I don't care how many sausages are in there."

He whined softly when she tugged him away. They walked back to Main Street and then another half a block to the municipal park. Two women were just ahead of her on the gravel pathway that ran the circumference of the green. They were ambling slowly and took up most of the path. PC started to step onto the grass to go around them, but her ears pricked up at their conversation.

"… terrible thing about the Afters. I've been meaning to give those girls a call," said the one in the light blue scarf and hat.

"Really, Sylvia? Isn't their going bankrupt a dream come true for Thorne?" A thick, shocking pink hoodie ensured this woman could be spotted by search and rescue at least a mile away.

"Don't get me started with that. He thinks that place would be the perfect Possumwood museum, filled, of course, with Marberger family heirlooms."

Sylvia Marberger? Silvia is Rose's sister-in-law. So, Sylvia is what, my aunt-in-law? Does that even count? She decided it didn't. Probably.

Pinky laughed. "A perfect excuse to redecorate."

"Are you kidding? There's so much stuff in storage. I can't even tell you–it's nuts." Sylvia shook her head. "He never had the slightest interest in his great-grandmother's old house until it got all fixed up. I told Thorne to leave those girls alone, but he goes by to pester them about selling every so often."

Aunt Lily and Uncle Cort had moved to Vermont almost as soon as they got married, and PC was only a toddler when that happened. She couldn't remember the last time she'd seen them, but she was still closer to them than she'd ever been to the Marbergers.

"They might do it, now." The pink hood bobbed.

"Lucky me. He'll probably try to get me to dress up in costume and lead tours around the museum."

They both chuckled, then Sylvia turned to her friend. "Wouldn't that be a sight? Humph. He can do that himself. But no, I was going to see if they needed anything, like a zero-interest loan to cover expenses for a few weeks until this blows over. Thorne has enough projects going on–he needs a museum like he needs a hole in his head. He'll delegate it to me, and I'm flat not interested."

Pinky laughed again. "How bad does he want this thing? You don't think he'd slip some tainted oysters into the buffet, do you?"

Sylvia did not laugh. "I don't believe my husband would deliberately kill anybody over real estate." Her tone was a warning.

Pinky fell silent. Cordite stopped to water the roses, and PC watched the two women stroll away from her.

Interesting. Sylvia didn't deny that Thorne would contaminate the buffet, just that she didn't think he'd intentionally kill *anyone.* Did he plan to just make people sick, then scoop up the property in the messy aftermath?

PC had passed the tower hundreds, maybe even thousands, of times. It stood in the park, a solitary turret without a castle. What was it for again? Some 1800s water project? Now, there was a new sign in front of it.

A black bat was caught mid-flight, wings outstretched on a pale-yellow background that made her think of the rising moon. The silvery lettering on the bat read:

Wings Over Possumwood

Bat Observation Point

March - September

"Huh." PC supposed there had always been bats in Possumwood. She'd just never noticed them. "C'mon, Cordie. You want a chew-chew?"

The dog pricked up his ears and wagged his tail. They headed back to Rose's house.

Cordite gnawed away on his fauxhide treat while PC's laptop booted up. She made herself some coffee and sat down. She had made a list of victims and potential suspects.

Even if there were a number of people who wanted to close down the Afters, she couldn't forget the diners who got sick. Would anybody want to put them out of commission?

Sam? She didn't have enough information. But he was a high school kid, so probably not.

Daisy? If she had any enemies, she hadn't mentioned them. And there was no way Daisy could stop herself from mentioning something like that. Was a Karla's Kurls customer so enraged by their haircut that they'd poison a buffet? Theoretically possible, but not very likely.

Drew? Again, she did not have enough information. But there didn't seem to be a high probability that someone would have a vendetta against a retired insurance agent and art gallery owner.

Woody? People can get furious when they're arrested. Some blame the cop who arrested them, instead of themselves for do-ing something arrestable. It was certainly possible that Woody had revenge-seeking felons on his heels but poisoning a buffet didn't feel like something the average impulse-control challenged crook would do. But it wasn't impossible.

The first guy to be affected. The one she tried to help. Beau Hopkins. Tran hadn't reported anything unusual about him. He owned the local nursery at the edge of town. Rose knew him and his wife, Janelle. He was most likely collateral damage.

But that grand jury witness, though.

Typing *Zev Daniels* into the search bar yielded tons of results. The most recent of which, reports of his untimely death, didn't add much to what she already knew. As she read further, though, she got a better idea of the man. He was the former Chief Financial Officer of the Noren Corporation, who resigned about the time that an investigative journalist published an exposé on Mob ties to the CEO, Gerald Stand. Daniels was not so much of a whistle blower as a deal maker–he'd sing like a worm-eating warbler about the financial shenanigans in exchange for a reduced sentence.

Who would want to kill him? Besides the thousands of people who lost huge chunks of their retirement funds that were invested in market darling Noren Corp., probably Gerald Stand and any of his syndicate connections. *Well, that narrows it down.*

Why was he not in protective custody? Or at the very least, have a security detail. Not hard to figure out he'd likely be a target if he were in a public place. So, how did he end up out in the sticks at a fatal brunch?

Chapter 10

ROSE'S VOICE CALLED from the back porch. "Primrose? Honey, can you run down to the store and get some more cat food?"

Really? Right now? "In a little bit."

"Alright, but don't leave it too late."

PC sighed. The interruption had derailed her train of thought. Might as well get it over with. "You want me to pick you up something for lunch while I'm out, Mama?"

"I'm good." Rose replied. "But if you just happen to drive by the Brisk Rib, and there's not a big line, I could do with a barbeque sandwich."

PC smiled to herself. *Never just say 'yes' when you can beat around the bush.*

She grabbed her keys. "Okay. Be back soon."

The cat food sat in the back seat, and the Rib was a block away. PC's phone chimed. She waited until she got inside and in line before she checked the message.

"You coming to darts? Drew had texted."

Is it Wednesday already? How did that happen? "Are you going to be allowed out for the evening?"

"Bringing Connor with me."

"Cool. See you then."

She wasn't really looking forward to being around Drew's son—he didn't seem to like her. Or it could be that his dad having female friends was what he didn't like. But she *was* looking forward to seeing the gallery owner. Their friendship had gotten comfortable in the short time PC had been in Possumwood. When Rose's hip replacement finished healing and PC went back to Houston, she'd miss him. She might still come for the Saturday art workshops at the gallery, though.

"Next!"

"Yes, ma'am. One barbecue sandwich and a Brisk Tater, no chives, to go, please."

After they finished their lunches, PC thought she would have some time to study her father's murder book. The one that had mysteriously appeared in the front seat of her car while she was at the police station, picking up Rocky after they'd dragged him in for questioning. She stood up.

"Honey, before you run off, could you help me order some flowers for Beau Hopkins' funeral? Mabel called me this morning and said they had released his body, so the services are going to be held on Saturday."

"What do you need help with?"

Rose drooped. "I can't read the numbers on my credit card so good anymore. I was gonna call up Pearlette's Petals and have her send somethin' out. That being said, Beau was an orchid grower—he was in the paper once for some international competition he'd won—so Janelle probably has more flowers than she can shake a stick at." She gave a little laugh. "Could you write down the card number and stuff on a piece of paper so I can read it?"

PC did as her mother asked, then retreated to her bedroom. She slid the burgundy three-ring binder out from under her bed and flipped through the pages, hoping a clue would spring out at her.

After the fabulous morning, a cold front had swept thunderstorms in during the afternoon. The lighting had passed, but it was still chilly and raining, so PC decided it was probably better to drive to the Biersal for darts. She picked up her keys.

Rocky sat on the couch with Cordite. She almost invited her brother to come with her, but decided against it. Someone should be around to look after Rose. And it might not be the best idea to take a recovering alcoholic to a bar.

"See you later," PC waved to the two of them as she left.

"Have fun, honey," Rose said from behind her Southern Living magazine.

As she pulled into the parking lot of the brew pub, she accidentally ran over a tiny corner of the yard of the man who was so irate about guests from the Afters driving on his grass. The Biersal driveway was at a weird angle, and it was hard to make the turn without either bowing out into oncoming traffic or cutting the corner. Since she usually walked, she never noticed before. The big rock she'd seen the neighbor and the backhoe crew putting into place earlier ensured she only skimmed the edge of the grass. *Interesting.*

The darts group lounged in its usual spot, glasses of beer in various states of consumption adorning the tables. Connor Berlusconi sat in the corner, away from everyone, looking at his phone.

Drew waved at her when the door opened, she waved back, then detoured to the bar to order before she joined the others.

The bartender reached for a glass. "Your usual?"

"Not tonight, Ken. Dr Pepper and… do you have any pretzels?"

"Not right now. There's more rising, though. They sell out as soon as they come out of the oven."

"I'm not surprised–they're so good."

"Thanks. They're Granny Zimmerman's secret recipe."

PC scanned the menu. "Guess I'll go with a large nachos." She handed him a twenty, then dropped some change into the tip jar.

He handed her the soda. "I'll bring the nachos out for you."

"Thanks."

She set her drink down at Drew's table and pulled up a stool. "How're you feeling?"

"I'm fine. Get out of breath a little easier than normal, but otherwise, it's like it never happened."

Jim Hargraves pulled his stool up to the tiny table. "PC, I want to apologize to you again for the incident the other day."

Drew sat up straighter. "What incident?"

Jim looked at the table. "Waitstaff–former waitstaff–was rude and unprofessional towards Rose."

PC reached for her drink. "You can pick your friends, but you can't pick your relatives, right?" She took a sip.

Jim looked over his shoulder at Connor. "He's not going to play?"

Drew followed his gaze. "Doesn't look like it."

Jim mimed holding a smartphone and tapping the screen. "Kids these days."

"Actually," Drew said, "he's a project manager, and he spends a lot of time with overseas clients and teams, using his phone."

PC's eyebrow arched up as she looked at the front door. "Speaking of kids these days."

Both men turned to see what she was looking at.

"She's got some nerve coming in here," Jim grumbled.

Sally, the City Café's newest former employee, took off her coat.

Winnie Hargraves came over and stood next to her husband. "What is she doing here?"

Bewildered, Drew asked, "Who is she?"

"Her name is Sally. She's the rude waitress from the City Café," PC mumbled.

Sally looked over at the Hargraves, and her eyes widened for a moment. Then she ignored them. *Pretending not to know us. Hard to blame her for that.*

"I hope she's not applying for a job." Winnie picked up her drink.

Jim shook his head and turned back toward the dart boards.

Sally sat at the bar, then the bartender brought her a glass of beer. PC saw her nachos sitting next to the cash register getting cold. But it gave her an idea.

"Be right back," PC said.

She got up and made a beeline for the congealing cheese and chips. Her eyes raked over Sally. The younger woman's eyes were red and puffy, and her skin was blotched with red.

"You okay, Sally?"

"What difference does it make to you?" she snapped.

PC shrugged. "You just look sad." She held out the paper box of nachos, and Sally accepted a sagging chip.

The former waitress chewed. and PC watched her for a few moments before she set the tray down on the bar and took a seat on the next barstool. "I know it can be tough when you're first out on your own."

Sally took another chip. Then another. And another. "Who doesn't send their kid money when they really need it?"

"I'm guessing your dad?"

"You got that right." She took a big gulp of beer, nacho cheese smearing on the glass. "Well, I'll show him. My boyfriend lives in Austin. I'll just move in with him." More beer and gooey chips.

How much did you have to drink before you got here? "Your dad doesn't like him?"

Sally's laugh was somewhere between a snort and a grunt. "My dad thinks I'm a virgin."

I bet he doesn't.

Sally picked up another flabby chip. "Daddy doesn't know, but I spent the entire weekend with Parker. Almost slept through my alarm Monday `cuz I didn't get home until three AM." A lopsided grin cracked her face.

"So, you were in Austin all weekend?"

Sally nodded, then lost her balance and almost fell off the barstool.

PC reached out to steady her. "That sounds fun."

"Yah. Sixth Street on Friday night. But then," Sally had another swallow of beer. "Sunday morning, we were going out to Marble Falls, and I got a flat on the stupid tollway. It took that guy so long to come out. And he didn't have to laugh at us because I didn't know there was a spare in the trunk."

"Hmmm." Calling for roadside assistance and being on the tollway would make Sally's story easy to prove (or disprove). PC mentally dropped her to the bottom of the suspect list.

She gazed at the matte skin that had formed on her drooping chips. Nachos are only edible when they're fresh and hot. "You know what? I'm going to leave these with you. They're waiting on me to start the dart game, so I'd better get back." PC stood up to leave.

"Fang oo." A curd of orange cheese dangled from her lips.

"Sure. Any time."

"Ha!" Winnie's dart was squarely in the middle of the narrow double ring under the eight. Bill Montoya and Mary Anne Mc-Donald, her fellow teammates, raised their glasses. Bill owned the local Ford dealership and Mary Anne ran a day care place.

"Losers buy the next round." Bill grinned.

Jim sulked. "Cricket next."

"Why not stick with 01?" Mary Anne asked.

While they squabbled over the next game, PC excused herself, partly because she needed the ladies' room, and partly because she wanted to check on Sally.

The young woman perched on her barstool, staring forlornly at her phone. Her glass was still around the same level as when she'd left Sally, and PC hoped it hadn't been re-filled. Ken Zimmerman wasn't just a bartender. He and his twin brother, Stan, owned the Biersal. He of all people would be aware of what could happen to bars that over-served customers.

The door opened and an older man came in. He gave Sally a quick once over before bellying up to the bar and ordering his own drink.

PC recognized him instantly. He was the Afters' irate neighbor with the big rock. *Perfect. Now I don't have to hunt him down.*

Chapter 11

"HEY, CLIFF!" CALLED a bearded man from one of four pool tables. "Could you get me another of them *Dark Half* IPAs while you're up there?"

The rock-placing neighbor nodded.

Drew interrupted her surveillance. "PC, you're up."

"What are we playing?"

"Cricket."

"Mmm." She preferred 01. Cricket was harder because you had to hit specific numbers, kind of like *Yahtzee!*, only with darts.

Fifteen seemed like a good choice. PC was well aware that her aim tended to skew low.

Thunk. Too low. She tripled into the two. May as well have missed the board.

Thunk. Too much over correction. Solidly in the ten. Still no good.

Thunk. She hadn't been aiming for the seventeen, but no one had to know that.

"One down, two to go." Jim raised his glass.

Bill stepped up to the line for his turn.

Drew had gone to the gents, and PC sat on his stool, where she could see Cliff and Beardo playing pool and downing brews. She thought a drink or two might lubricate Cliff's jaws–it usually worked that way. But she didn't want to try talking to him if he was flat out drunk. No point in that. And she couldn't just wander up and say, "Hey, Cliff. How's your new rock?"

A copy of the local newspaper, the Possumwood Press, lay on the next table over. It was opened to an obituary of the man who'd died at the brunch.

Beau Hopkins, owner of the Elite Orchids nursery and internationally acclaimed orchid grower, has entered the Eternal Kingdom. He is survived by his children, Ben and Sara Beth, his much beloved wife Janelle Hopkins, and his aunt, Mabel Radcliffe.

A list of relatives who had pre-deceased him followed, but the details for when the service would be held were pending, based on when the Medical Examiner released his body. PC felt a twinge of guilt. She'd done everything she could, she told herself. Still, she felt bad that she hadn't been able to save him. Beneath the obituary, a headline about the sale of Elite Orchids for half a million dollars caught PC's eye. The article was folded under, out of sight.

Mary Ann's voice startled her before she could open the paper to read it. "What? … okay… I'll be right there."

Everyone in the group turned to her.

"I'm sorry, guys. My mom's dog got out, and I have to go help her catch him before he gets into the neighbors' chickens. They've already threatened to shoot him if he comes on the property."

Bill always brought her to darts, but PC wasn't sure if they were a couple or simply good friends. Maybe it was a little of both. They grabbed their gear and left.

"I'm really tired," Winnie said, not so subtly elbowing her husband.

"I was hoping we could have a quick game of 01. You and me against Drew and PC."

Winnie made a Steven Spielberg production of yawning and stretching. "I'm really sleepy. It was a long day at the Café."

Jim sighed, resigned to his fate. He glanced up at the bar. Sally was still there, and the corners of his mouth turned down.

"Well, good night, then." He packed up both their sets of darts into matching holographic cases.

Oddly, Cliff looked over at their table, craning his neck and swiveling his head.

"Night," Drew and PC said, almost in unison.

Winnie grinned at them. "Have fun."

"Of course." PC replied.

She watched the Hargraves walk out, obviously ignoring Sally. But the waitress' head drooped onto her chest as she stared at her phone on the bar.

"So," Drew nodded toward the dartboard. "You wanna…?"

"How good are you at 8 Ball?"

"Pool? Why do you ask?"

"Just thought we'd try something different."

He looked at her for a long moment, as if trying to read her intentions. "I have played before."

"Let's do it."

He paid for the rack and balls from the bartender while she got their drinks refilled. Connor was still in the corner with his phone, nursing a dark beer and a basket of fries. PC hoped he didn't get antsy and decide to go home anytime soon. She suspected that Winnie had forgotten about Drew's son when her sudden fit of 'exhaustion' had taken hold.

"It's been a while since I've played." PC racked the balls. "I'll try not to hurt anybody."

Drew's eyebrows shot up. "Thanks for the warning. Do you want to pick your own cue, or you want me to grab one for you?"

"You can get it."

The cues were in a large wooden frame on the same wall of the brew pub as the dartboards, but closer to the door. PC watched Drew select the pool sticks while she listened for any scraps of conversation between Cliff and Beardo. They communicated mostly through grunts, however.

Drew rolled the cues on a nearby table, presumably to check for straightness. *Good grief. I'm not trying to win a tournament. I just want an excuse to talk to Cliff.* He returned and handed her a stick. "You racked. I'll break."

"Sure."

He set the plastic triangle on the edge of the table and positioned the cue ball in front of the apex of the triangle of balls. After pumping his stick arm a few times, he struck the glossy white ball, and the others scattered across the green felt. No balls found a pocket.

PC took her turn but failed miserably to sink the orange five.

Drew lined up. "One-ball in the corner pocket." The yellow ball disappeared into the pocket, followed by the white one.

"A scratch? Really?" He surveyed the table before setting the white ball down on the opposite side.

"Six in the back corner."

This shot misfired, and the cue ball glanced off the fourteen, sending it rolling meekly against the rail.

PC lined up her shot. "Eleven, side." She drew back her cue and met resistance.

"Ow! Watch it!" Beardo rubbed his ample gut.

PC cringed. "Sorry!"

He shook his head. "No, it's my fault."

"I really didn't mean to jab you." She moved over a little and realigned her shot.

The cue struck the ball at the bottom, causing it to pop into the air, and nearly hit Drew. Cliff and Beardo snickered behind her. The ball dropped to the wooden floor, sounding like a cannonball had just fallen through the ceiling.

"Are you sure you want to keep playing?" Drew leaned over to pick up the cue ball.

"Sure. I'm just getting warmed up. I warned you I was rusty."

PC didn't injure any bystanders during the rest of the game. She took it as a win. It took a while, but she finally hit her stride and got a few balls in. Drew repeatedly called difficult shots and missed them. Stripes and solids took their sweet time falling into their pockets, but were finally tucked in. PC won, but she had a sneaking suspicion Drew had let her.

Cliff cleared his throat. "Y'all got some interestin' skills over there."

"Ah… thanks?" PC wiped pool cue chalk off her hands and onto her pants.

With a sideways glance at Cliff, Beardo said, "For our own safety, we was thinkin' we'd ask y'all to play over here with us."

"Maybe." Drew looked from one to the other. "Stakes?"

Beardo tapped his cue on the table. "Somethin' friendly. Loser buys the next round of drinks."

"Well, um…" Cliff babbled, then held up his arm to reveal a nasty, bruised scrape that ran from the back of his wrist all the way to the first knuckle of his middle finger. Fresh blood was oozing out of the wound "Got it trapped between the chain and the rock. It's kinda startin' to shake. Not sure I'm up for another round."

Perfect! PC wanted to talk to Cliff, not pretend to enjoy another round of pool. She hoped Drew wouldn't press him into joining.

"Okay. You and me." Drew smiled innocently at Beardo.

"I was done anyway," PC said.

She put away her cue and stood next to Cliff, sipped her now watered-down Dr Pepper. The detective regarded Cliff's injured hand lying on the table. "You should have that looked at."

"It's nothin'." He moved it into his lap.

PC shrugged. "I was at the Afters the other day and saw you putting that big rock up in your yard. That's an unusual design choice. Where did you get it?"

"Heh. My sister's husband has a landscapin' business in Houston. I got sick uh people drivin' over the corner of my grass."

Beardo broke and sank four balls in quick succession.

"I expect that will keep 'em off the lawn." PC set down the watery drink. It was probably too late in the day for sugary caffeine, anyway.

Beardo missed the ten ball.

Drew walked around the table, deciding his first move.

Cliff wiped his forehead. "But it doesn't. Not really. I thought it was all them folks from the Afters. Ain't nobody there, and still people are forever in my yard. I kinda feel sorry for them gals, now."

The cue ball clicked against the green solid and it rolled into the side pocket.

"Oh?"

"My wife loved that place. We went to every event. Ain't been in there since she died year before last. But if they go outta business. Who knows what's gonna be next? I wish they had never got hold of them tainted oysters."

Click. Click. Click.

Every solid ball fell into a pocket. Drew looked straight into Beardo's face while he sank the eight ball.

"Good night almighty!" Beardo set his beer down hard on the table.

"What?" Cliff asked.

"Not you."

PC's brows furrowed, perplexed.

Cliff chuckled. "Gets confusing, sometimes, when your last name's Goodnight. Didn't know we'd challenged some pool sharks to a game. Glad it wasn't for nothin' more than drinks."

"Well, you're in luck there. I'm done for the night." Drew set his cue on the table.

The front door swung open, and a tall young man swept in.

"Parker!" Sally slid off her barstool to embrace him.

"I got here as fast as I could. Are you okay?"

She started sobbing. He put his arms around her.

PC struck Cliff Goodnight from her suspect list. Truth be told, he wasn't very high on it to begin with. Who was left? Thorne Marberger, the crazy petition lady–Mabel Radcliffe, and a completely unknown subject who might have been out to silence grand jury witness Zev Daniels. That last one was well beyond her current investigative capacity, however.

Drew returned from putting away his cue, then he put the balls and rack on the tray. He leaned backward, stretching, and stood with his hands on their table.

"You said you were ready to go. Did you need a ride?"

"No. I drove. But thanks. You look like you should probably call it a night, too. No sense in over-doing it."

PC thought she detected a hint of disappointment in his eyes, but it could have been a trick of the dim light. "I'll see you on Saturday. And I have a question: where did you learn to play pool like that?"

He grinned. "I'll walk you to your car."

The rain had picked up, and PC frowned. At least there was a wide overhang that would cover them for about half of their journey to the parking lot.

"My cousin." Drew said. "He was crazy about trick pool shots. Taught me everything I know. I even managed to pay for all my college textbooks and then some, playing pool during the summer."

"You're full of surprises."

"Good."

He produced a collapsible umbrella from his coat pocket and opened it at the end of the overhang. They huddled under it and walked awkwardly to her car, nearly tripping each other twice because they were so close, and their steps were out of sync. He held the brolly over the door while she got in.

"Thanks."

He bowed slightly. "My pleasure."

"You just got out of the hospital. Get out of this rain. I'll see you Saturday."

He laughed. "Night."

She started the engine as she watched him walk back to the building. For someone who seemed so bookish and artsy, it was hard to believe the story of his sharking pool. But she'd seen it with her own eyes.

"What other secrets do you have, Drew Berlusconi?"

Chapter 12

SATURDAY AFTERNOON WAS as spectacular as Wednesday afternoon had been dismal. The sun was bright, for February, and according to PC's car, it was a cool 65 degrees—almost too pretty of a day to spend indoors. Still, she was looking forward to the acrylics class, and she'd arrived early enough to hang out and chat with Drew beforehand.

A familiar face stood in front of a large watercolor near the front door. Sylvia Marberger. PC pondered the best approach to see if she could get this woman to talk.

"Sylvia?"

Marberger whipped her head around. She studied PC's face for several long moments. "You're that Donovan girl?" She snapped her fingers twice. "Marigold. No. Lavender? Primrose! Lily's niece?"

Girl? "I go by PC, though."

Sylvia's eyes traveled the length of PC's body and back up again. "There is a strong family resemblance, that's for sure. You know, we were just skiing with her and Cort last month in Aspen."

"Sounds like a fun trip. How is Aunt Lily?"

"Fine. She said your mother broke her hip. I was sorry to hear about that. I did send her some flowers."

"Thank you. I'm in town taking care of her until the hip replacement surgery heals."

"That's very good of you." Sylvia shifted her weight away from PC.

I'm losing her. "Well, she has a lot of animals that need feeding. Are you doing the acrylics workshop this afternoon?"

"Oh, Lord, no. We just bought a condo in Houston because Thorne's there so much. I'm looking for some art for the place."

Set the hook. "Yes. Renetta was at Mama's house the other day, bird dogging properties for him."

Sylvia raised her eyes to the ceiling. "I'm sorry about that. That woman is like the Hounds of Hell—she won't stop chasing after somebody once she's got 'em in her sights."

"She did say Thorne was trying to buy up some land around town. For investment purposes, of course."

"He always has some project or another in the works."

Reel her in. "Oh? Like the Afters?"

Sylvia took a step backward and blinked rapidly. "Did Renetta say that?"

"Renetta? No. She's a true professional. But I wondered, since he's interested in buying properties, and they may have to sell, given that terrible shellfish poisoning incident."

Sylvia shook her head, and it made PC think of a bobble-head statue on a windy day. "Thorne's been talking about buying that place for years—got it in his head he wants to make it a museum. He does not have time for that. And neither do I. He's only half serious about it—he wouldn't know what to do with a museum if it bit him on the butt. Besides, he likes their food too much. We never miss one of their events."

"So, you were at the bunch Sunday?"

"Of course. What did I just say?" Sylvia shifted again. "Glad neither of us likes oysters."

Wilma, the acrylics instructor, strolled in.

"Hey, Drew!"

The instructor and gallery owner gave each other air kisses, and then she traipsed back to the classroom. PC knew she was running out of time.

PC ran a hand through her short hair. "You don't, by any chance, remember what you ate, do you?"

"What kind of question is that?"

Three ladies, PC's fellow classmates, came into the gallery. She glanced at her watch.

"I know it sounds weird, but I really want to know."

"Why?"

"I don't think it was the oysters."

Two more ladies came in and made their way to the teaching room. She'd have to follow them soon.

"It wasn't the French toast, strawberries, and whipped cream, because I had all of those, and I'm fine. And Thorne had an omelet and three Napoleons."

She had the strawberries? Obviously, she didn't get there after people started getting sick. "You must have been an early bird."

"Thorne always wants to be there when the doors open. For anything. Gotta have first pick."

"So, you'd already left before the pandemonium started."

Sylvia looked forlornly at the painting and sighed. "Yes."

"I'm glad that you and Thorne are okay. It was pretty scary when Daisy and Drew were both in the hospital. I've got to get to my class. It was good to see you."

A curt nod was Sylvia's response.

"You'd better hurry—Wilma doesn't like stragglers." Drew waved her toward the back.

A man stood looking at the expensive Patrick Daun oil painting that Drew had displayed near the front of the gallery. She was sure she'd seen him somewhere before. One of Rose's friends? Seemed a bit young for that. Now it was going to bug her until she remembered. But for now, Wilma would not wait.

PC heard Drew ask, "Is there anything in particular you were looking for?"

"No, thanks. I just needed to get out of my hotel room and get some air."

"Ahem." Wilma cleared her throat as she eyed PC. "Please take a seat so we can get started."

The workshop focused on hue and value. PC painted a strawberry because she couldn't think of anything else. Almost white to almost black, cheerful red in the middle, highlight and shadow. She wasn't entirely happy with the bright-to-dark green tuft of greenery on top. The fat stem was too round—the whole thing reminded her of an octopus.

A shellfish.

The strawberries either weren't poisoned at all, or the STX was added after the Marbergers left.

Chapter 13

WHEN PC ARRIVED back at Rose's house, carrying her mostly dry canvas, she was surprised to see her mother sitting on the porch talking to someone. It took her a minute to recognize Mabel Radcliffe. *What is she doing here?*

The detective glanced over her shoulder, wondering if Hiro's car was in front of the Youn's house, but the street was empty. She hoped she wouldn't need backup.

"Primrose, you remember Mabel from the hospital the other day, don't you?"

"I do."

Mabel dropped her head and looked at the painted concrete floor.

"She stopped by to see how Daisy was doing."

"That was nice of her." PC held the canvas between her and Mabel like a shield.

Mabel looked up. "Have you been at a garage sale?"

"Painting workshop."

"Oh." Mabel fidgeted with her purse strap.

Rose gave the canvas a quick once over. "I think your big strawberry looks very nice, honey."

Thanks. I'll run in and stick it on the fridge. "I'm glad you like it."

Mabel took a deep breath and let it out. "I'm terribly sorry about making such a ruckus at the hospital. My doctor was tinkering with my medication—I'm afflicted with two kinds of arthritis." She flexed her knobby fingers. "And a heart condition. Sometimes... there are interactions. I had a bad reaction for a few days. Phineas took me to Dr. Chowdry on Monday, and she remedied the situation. It's just embarrassing. I'm not normally... so undignified."

The only Phineas that PC could come up with off the top of her head was Phineas Taylor Barnum. That might explain the three-ring circus she presided over at the hospital.

"He's her neighbor," Rose pointed out.

P. T. Barnum? "Hmmm." PC relaxed her grip on the canvas, and it dipped down, the corner of it nearly grazing the floor.

"Don't you know the mayor? Phineas Scott?" Rose's raised eyebrows were almost comical.

How should I know that? "Oh, okay. Mayor's neighbor. Got it."

"I hope I didn't make too bad of an impression. I mean, I don't know those girls. I've never even been to the Afters. I'm just... so embarrassed."

"It's okay." PC gave her best reassuring smile. "This kind of stuff happens. When they open back up, you should go."

"I do not patronize establishments that sell alcohol." She crossed her hands in her lap. "Nor do I eat at restaurants that serve seafood. I have a terrible allergy to shellfish. It runs in our family."

Before PC could respond, Rose started grinning and waving. A glance over her shoulder showed PC that Terry Gillespie was sauntering up her mother's walkway.

Mabel clutched her purse and stood up so abruptly she startled Chirp, the plump calico who had been snoozing on a nearby bench. She jumped onto the table in her mad dash to escape from Mabel and nearly knocked a vase of roses onto Rose's lap.

"It looks like your gentleman caller's here." Mabel's nostrils flared, and her lips pursed in disapproval.

"Yes. You enjoy the rest of your day, now. Thank you for stoppin' by." Rose got out of her chair and leaned on her cane.

The screen door snapped against the door frame in Mabel's wake. She could have waited another two seconds and held it for Terry, but she minced past him, prim as Jane Austen's grandmother.

"Afternoon, Mabel!" he called after her.

She paused but didn't turn around.

Terry's Old Spice cologne preceded him as he pulled open the screen door and swept onto the porch, planting a kiss on Rose's cheek. She giggled.

Get a room. No! No rooms. Stay arm's length apart. PC leaned her strawberry portrait against the wall and crossed her arms.

"So, Terry. We haven't had a chance to get to know each other."

Rose almost dropped her cane. "Primrose!"

"Rose, it's okay." Terry adjusted his collar. "Your daughter is just looking out for you."

"I'm old enough to look out for myself." She plopped into her chair.

PC winced, willing her mother's hip to stay in place. "Mama! Please be more careful. You don't want to dislodge that brand new titanium hip, now do you?"

"I don't need a nursemaid!"

"Ladies!" Terry gestured as if he were pushing something away from his navel with both hands, then he opened up his arms. "Let's take a deep breath and relax."

PC flicked her wrist so she could see her FlitBit. "I need to go feed the animals."

She scooped up her painting and stalked to her own room. After leaning it carefully against the far wall, she slipped on a jacket and trudged outside, taking Cordite with her. As she scooped the donkeys' grain, it suddenly hit her.

She remembered where she'd seen the man in the art gallery.

Chapter 14

THAT MAN HAD been at the Afters when PC and Rose's entourage arrived. She'd watched him from the omelet line. His being alone at the romance-based brunch had struck her as odd at the time. Later, at the gallery, he'd said he needed to get out of his hotel room. Could he be an assassin who binged on the buffet and then terminated Zev Daniels before he could testify?

But that made no sense. A hit man would neutralize his target and leave, not hang around town visiting the shops for a week. Well, a *professional* assassin would hit the highway. There were a lot of yahoos who thought they were professional quality but were far from it. Sometimes the Dunning-Kruger Effect is a detective's best friend—the dumber they are, the smarter they think they are. There might be enough of a draw in Possumwood to attract day-trippers from the Houston area for a day, or even a weekend, but a whole week? Why was he here?

Eeeyahw! Eeeeeeeeeyaw! Yahyahyahyah!

Maaaaa! Mmmmmaaa!

"Okay, okay! Dinner's coming. Jeez."

She poured the smaller buckets of feed into rubber tubs, one each for Guinevere, Arthur, and Hazel. While they had their noses in the troughs, she put flakes of hay into the racks. But she mentally rehashed her list of suspects.

Suspect 1. Cliff Goodnight was a grumpy old widower whose wife had loved the Afters. He said he hadn't been there since she died two years ago. He'd gotten his brother-in-law to put up a big rock for him, hoping to encourage people to stay off the grass. Never a strong suspect, and even weaker when he credibly denied being there.

Suspect 2. Mabel Radcliffe was an interesting character. The prudish aunt of one of the victims who had a prescription drug interaction that sent her off her rocker. Could she have sprinkled STX in the food and quietly left? Did she hate the Afters more than she loved her nephew? Or did she have a grudge against him? His wife? Or was she too addled to know what she was doing? Perhaps, but that poison's not a simple thing to acquire. This murder took advanced, intricate planning. Unless she just happened to have some in her kitchen cupboard while she was on her medication-fueled rampage. Possible, but not likely.

PC started to fasten the door on the chicken coop. The hens were pretty good about putting themselves to bed at night. She just had to lock the doors against any varmints on the hunt for a free chicken dinner.

Then something caught her eye. Or failed to catch her eye. The big orange hen, Clementine, was missing. Pavarotti, the rooster, perched alone on an upper bench, unruffled, taking up all the space for himself. Twilight had started to seep in from the trees, but it wasn't dark enough to need a flashlight yet.

Rose would be upset to know one of her beloved hens was AWOL, so PC used her inside voice, hoping to fly under her mother's radar. "Clementine! Here chicky chicky!" *Do chickens come when you call them? Without the feed?* She didn't want to get the others stirred up.

PC made a circuit of the outer perimeter of the pen, calling softly for Clementine. Cordite assisted by snuffling in the bushes. She had made her way around the property that wasn't visible from the front porch. Once she came passed the corner of the garage, she might have some 'splainin' to do.

Cordite yipped, and something flapped.

"Oh, Clementine. What have you done to yourself?"

The bird had trapped her leg in a rusty piece of wire, and in her efforts to get free, gotten one wing caught in a holly bush. PC freed the wing first, then carefully unwrapped the wire, while Clementine unhelpfully jerked her legs as if she were trying to run. A final kick shook off the binding.

There was an explosion of orange feathers as Clementine frantically flapped her wings, slapping PC in the face and head. She launched herself into the air and away from the startled detective. PC had forgotten chickens could fly.

Miss Clementine flew straight to the coop, and with much cackling and crooning, tucked herself in bed. By the time PC made it back to lock up, Clementine had nestled in with the other hens and they quietly chirped and gossiped together. Pavarotti ignored them.

"What kind of husband are you? Your wife goes missing and you don't even care. You're safe in here with all the grain. And the other women." The rooster ignored her, too.

Speaking of roosters…

Suspect 3. Thorne Marberger. Even though his brother was married to her aunt, that aunt lived in Vermont, and PC remembered seeing her not more than a dozen times. The Marbergers didn't mix outside their social circle, although they checked on Rose from time to time as a favor to Cort and Lily. The detective didn't know either Thorne or Sylvia particularly well. She'd overheard Sylvia's conversation with her friend, and she believed that Sylvia didn't want the Afters. Thorne? Not enough information.

He was buying up properties. He wanted the Afters property, but did he want it badly enough to spike the brunch buffet on the way out the door?

Suspect 4. Sally Rivers. She blamed Caitlyn and Simone for firing her, and she had anger management issues. She also had an alibi. Roadside assistance was changing a tire for her in Austin at the time.

Suspect 5. The unknown subject. There were probably a lot of people who did not want Zev Daniels to testify. Frankly, if that was the case, PC had precious few resources to investigate it, and it was probably best not to. At least, if she didn't want to risk putting herself on the killer's to-do list. Was the stranger she'd seen at the Afters, then again in Drew's gallery, responsible? It didn't seem likely—he'd be crazy to hang around town.

Unless…

She texted Tran. "Hey. How's the buffet murder investigation going?"

"Slow."

"Do you know if Zev was meeting any locals?"

"No. Y"

"Saw man eating alone at buffet. Seemed odd. Saw him again yesterday. Probably nothing. Unless he is poisoner."

Her phone rang. "Hey, Tran."

"Why do you think the dude might be the poisoner?"

PC leaned on the board fence. "It's probably nothing. But I did notice him at the buffet. Alone at Valentine's brunch, playing with his phone. Then he was at Drew's gallery this afternoon. What is there in Possumwood in February that would make a tourist want to hang around for a week?"

"Can't think of anything."

"If he did sprinkle some STX on the food, it makes no sense that he'd stay around, either. Unless there was someone here he was trying to find. Somebody could be in real danger."

"How do you know he's been here all week?"

"I saw him at the brunch, then he told Drew he needed to get some fresh air because he was feeling cooped up after being in his hotel all week."

"What does he look like?"

PC gave him the man's description.

"I'll be on the lookout."

"Be careful."

"Always."

She disconnected and put her phone in her back pocket while she checked the water tank. A gentle caress slipped up the back of her thigh to her right butt cheek.

"Hey!" She whipped around to see Hazel standing there with her tongue sticking out.

The phone was sticky with goat slobber and grain fragments.

"What is wrong with you, you crazy goat?"

Cordite barked from the other side of the fence.

PC wiped the screen as best she could with her shirt. She hadn't intended to unlock it, but her finger grazed the fingerprint sensor. As she wiped, she accidentally clicked on an ad. An aggressive male voice boomed out of the speaker.

"You need a quick and easy divorce? Call my office—"

Ugh. She stopped the video and shut down the phone. *Why did I start getting these ads now?*

Something crawled across her chest and she snatched at it, hoping to stop a bug invasion of her brassiere. Instead of a six-legged interloper, she pulled out one of Clementine's orange feathers. She looked at it for a moment, and then it hit her.

I've been looking at this completely wrong. I know who the killer is now.

Chapter 15

PC WHISTLED FOR Cordite and he met her at the gate. She checked the front porch for Rose and Terry, but they'd gone inside. She couldn't blame them—it was getting chilly. Murmurs and guffaws came from the living room, so PC expected to find them there. She hadn't expected to see them playing dominoes with her brother at a card table.

"Hey, Rocky. Didn't see you come home."

He patted the couch to encourage Cordite to jump up. "Yeah. Just got here." He gestured to the free side of the table. "Mexican Train?"

"Next time—I have to finish something right now. C'mon Cordie. Let's get your dinner."

"Your loss."

Toenails clicked on the faded yellow linoleum as Cordite followed her into the kitchen. PC dumped the wet food into his dish. After she rinsed the can and dropped it into the recycling bin, she called Daisy.

"Hey, Dais. How you feeling?"

"Mostly alright. Kinda tired. Is everything okay with Mama?" Alarm crept into her voice.

"Mama's fine. She's got a game of dominoes going right now."
PC sat down at the kitchen table. "I needed to reconfirm something with you. What did you eat at the Afters?"

"Really? This is why you're calling me on a Saturday night?"

PC could hear the implied *Why don't you have a date?* but she
shook it off. "Yes. It's important."

"Fine. I had French toast with those little sausages. Green salad. Cheesy potatoes."

"What about the strawberries?"

"I started to take a bite of one, but then I noticed there was a
little green worm on the stem, so I left the rest. They didn't smell
ripe, anyway."

"So, you didn't actually eat any strawberries?"

"That's what I just said."

"Did you eat anything else?"

Silence.

"Daisy? I'm not the diet police. It's really important. Please."

A deep sigh hissed through the speaker. "I had some chocolate
mousse. They're famous for it, you know. I just—"

"Thank you. Have a good evening. Bye."

She tapped Tran's icon from the list of call log.

"This better be good. We're at *Truffles!* having dinner."

"I think I know who poisoned the buffet."

"Oh?"

"Pick me up at 12:30 tomorrow. Personal car, not your squad."

"Flowers?" Tran asked as she wrestled the vase of various stemmed roses and fern fronds into the car.

"Yeah. Everything here is closed on Sunday—I'm lucky Mama never got around to pruning her rose bushes."

"So, what's your plan?"

"I'll call you and put you on mute, but leave the phone on speaker. Then I'll turn on the voice recorder."

"You need a warrant for that."

"Correction. *You* need a warrant for that. I'm a private citizen, and as long as at least one party knows the conversation is being recorded, it's perfectly legal. You're my backup if things go south. Hence the speaker."

"If you're wrong…"

"I'm not."

"Oh." Tran stopped at a light. "Did I tell you that Cliff Goodnight confessed to throwing the brick through the window at the Afters? He was already carrying a grudge, and Mabel Radcliffe came by with her petition and got him all riled up. He was so embarrassed that he offered to pay to replace the window and have his brother-in-law do some hardscaping for them."

"Hardscaping?"

"Well, Simone said they were thinking about putting in a flagstone patio in the back, with big flowerbeds built in."

"Huh." The last thing on PC's mind was landscaping.

Tran pulled up in front of a cheery white bungalow with a fake wishing well, the bucket filled with red begonias, in the front yard.

Magenta azaleas were just starting to pop, vibrant against the pale siding. A cream-colored sign swung slightly in the breeze. 'FOR SALE' was emblazoned in bright red, while 'Renetta Sherman, Realtor' and her phone number were in a tasteful sepia.

It didn't take long to get the phones set up, and PC opened the door.

"Be careful."

"Always."

She struggled out of the car with the vase, trying not to crush the blossoms against the gate frame. The concrete path curved gently toward the wishing well, and it only took PC a few seconds to reach the beveled glass door. She rang the bell.

A figure moved behind the glass. The clicking of heels on wood got louder. The door did not open.

"Yes? Can I help you?"

"Mrs. Hopkins? It's PC Donovan. Rose's daughter? She sent me by to give you our deepest condolences."

"Thank you. I'm sorry, but I'm very busy."

"Yes, ma'am. I have some flowers for you. Fresh cut from Mama's garden."

The door opened and PC stepped forward. Instinctively, Janelle Hopkins moved out of the way.

"Those are very nice roses. Tell your mother I said thank you."

Two large suitcases and a carry on sat in the hall. "We're so sorry to have missed Beau's funeral. With Daisy recovering from being in the hospital and all…"

Janelle clung to the door, but PC wormed her way inside.

"Yes. I understand. Now, if you'll—"

PC moved deeper into the foyer and planted herself in front of a portrait of Beau, Janelle, and two young children. It had the yellowish tinge of an old photo.

"You know, I really did try to help him. When he collapsed on the way to the restrooms. I was the one who kept his airway clear until EMS arrived. He was terrified."

"Um... I..."

"Cute kids. They must be in college now."

"Sarah Beth's already graduated. Ben is... look, I—"

"Losing their father must have been a terrible shock to them. They probably didn't even care about the nursery business."

She huffed out a breath. "That was all Beau's."

"Rare orchids, right? Those are so much work."

Janelle let go of the door. "Tell me about it. That's all he seemed to care about anymore."

PC let her eyes wander to the luggage, then snapped them back to the pictures lining the entryway. One was a framed cover of *Orchids Today*, featuring a stunning flower with fringed edges that looked like the wing feathers of a flying bird. The petals were blue in the center and faded to white. Text at the bottom read, 'Beau Hopkins Dazzles with Egret Hybrids.' Janelle followed PC's eyes. "That magazine. Once his flower made the cover, that was it. Nothing else mattered—he had to get another cover. He was obsessed."

"I'm sure that wasn't easy."

"Easy? I worked my fingers to the bone to keep a roof over our heads and food on the table. He sold a few plants here and there to make room in the greenhouse, but he stopped treating the business like a business. When that Japanese company came and wanted to buy some blue egrets, he told them to take a hike. They offered $30,000. So much money, and he threw it away like it was nothing." Janelle pursed her lips.

PC nodded but said nothing.

"I just couldn't take it anymore. No sane person would put plants over family."

"You didn't really mean to hurt anyone else, did you?" PC's voice was soothing.

"Of course not. I accidentally dropped the vial into the mousse and—" Janelle gave a little snort and shook her head. "You figured it out, didn't you? What gave me away?"

"Nothing, at first. I was sure that either Zev Daniels or the Afters itself was the intended victim. Daniels was supposed to testify before a grand jury, and there were a few people who seemed interested in running the Reynolds ladies out of business. But I just couldn't get the facts to line up with either scenario. Turns out that Daniels had already finished his testimony, so the cat was long out of the bag. But the oysters weren't poisoned—it was the chocolate mousse. That puzzled me for a long time. Then yesterday, Beau's aunt dropped in on my mother and mentioned that shellfish allergies ran in their family. If he never ate shellfish, only someone close to him would know that. I'm guessing you intended to sprinkle a little on the oysters so everyone would think it was just a bad batch of seafood, but then you messed up and spilled the whole vial in the mousse. Am I right?"

Janelle scowled, her chest heaving with angry breaths.

PC continued. "I'd seen the newspaper headline about the sale of the orchid nursery and thought nothing of it. And then one of Mama's chickens got caught in the blooming holly bushes and

I had to go search for her while the rooster sat in the coop, safe and warm, with all the food and the other hens. He clearly had his priorities. If a raccoon or coyote happened by and helped itself… well, he was prepared to make that sacrifice—he had what he wanted. Beau was not going to sell the nursery, and you couldn't divorce him without giving up that money. You had 500,000 reasons to kill him. Plus, whatever his life insurance paid out. And if his death was accidental? Well, you just doubled your money."

"You're right. Now prove it."

"I think I can.

"I doubt that. I can't believe a chicken is what put it together for you." Janelle shook her head. "Did it not occur to you if I were willing to get rid of my husband that I'd have no qualms about killing you? It's nothing personal. But I have a plane to catch."

Janelle dropped a hand into her purse. Tran burst through the glass door, weapon drawn.

"Drop it!"

Janelle hesitated, weighing her options.

"Hands where I can see them. Now."

She tossed a small handgun toward PC, where it bounced harmlessly on the faux Persian rug.

"Yes, Janelle. It did occur to me that you might try something."

Tran cuffed Janelle and called for investigators.

Chapter 16

"Mama, you about ready? The party starts in thirty minutes." PC stood in front of an ornate mirror on the living room wall.

It was Friday, and all of Possumwood was invited Happily Ever Afters' official grand re-opening bash. Simone and Caitlyn had specifically included the county health inspectors.

"Almost," Rose called from her bathroom. "Just puttin' on my lipstick."

Rocky lounged on the couch. "I've *been* ready."

"Good. Can you take Cordie out to pee?"

"Didn't he go out with you when you fed the critters?"

"That was over an hour ago. Please? I want to make sure he's completely drained—it may be a while before we get back."

PC could hear the frown in his voice. "Fine. C'mon, Cordite."

The back screen door snapped behind them, and she evaluated her image in the glass. She was in reasonably good shape, but gravity was not her friend, although it had been kinder to her than many others. The dress, until Thursday, had been in her closet in her Houston home. It was a long way to go to pick up a dress, but she checked on the house weekly, anyway. A yard service was keeping the lawn and shrubs trimmed, and a neighbor was keeping an eye on the place, alarm company notwithstanding. It had hit her hard this trip. How much she missed her own home. The doctor had said it would take at least three months for Rose's hip replacement to heal fully. She was two months into it. PC could be home in April, if everything went well.

Pining over her house wasn't doing anybody any good. There was a celebration to go to.

The screen door slammed again, followed by the sound of Cordite lapping water. Rose came out of her bedroom in a red sequined cocktail dress and sexy white orthopedic shoes. The porch screen slapped against the frame and someone tapped on the front door.

PC tugged at the neckline of her dress. "Let's go."

Terry waited for them on the porch. "Rose, my darling, you look mahvelous!"

"So do you, sweet baboo."

They both chuckled.

PC jangled the car keys. "Mama, please! Can we just go? We still have to pick up Justice."

Rose tucked her hand into the crook of Terry's arm. "Come on."

They got into PC's SUV. Rocky sat up front with PC, so he took custody of Rose's cane.

Once they got out of the driveway, PC said, "Could someone text Justice to tell her we'll be there in about ten minutes?"

Let her chaperone these two. What are they? Teenagers?

Justice was waiting for them in front of the long driveway to her house, and they proceeded to the Afters. PC was delighted to see that the parking lot was packed.

"Let me drop you off at the door, and I'll go park." She pulled up at the entrance and Rocky helped Rose and company out of the back seat, then the detective parked the car.

As PC moved up the walkway to the restored Victorian, she almost felt like she'd slipped into another time. Kind of like at Disneyland, where the "lands" aren't real, but it's easy to pretend they are, just for a little while.

"Wow!"

PC turned to see Drew coming over to her.

"You look great! You should wear dresses more often."

She gave his sport coat and button-down shirt—with no tie—a quick once over. "You clean up pretty well yourself. I was expecting you to be inside—I dropped the crowd off at the door."

Drew fell into step with PC. "I know. I saw them. Thought I'd wait for you out here."

A doorman in a tailcoat opened the glass and iron door and they stepped into the foyer, which opened on the grand ballroom. Last time PC had seen it, paramedics were loading people onto stretchers. She liked this look much better. Soft amber lights reminded her of pictures she'd seen of gas lamps. A string quartet in the corner played a waltz, but there were far too many people milling around for anyone to dance. PC did not see that as a bad thing. She saw Rose talking with Hilda Wilson, Woody's mother.

PC and Drew approached the group. She saw no sign of Woody. "Hello, Mrs. Wilson. How've you been?"

"Primrose! Dear, it's good to see you outside of the hospital."

"Yes. You, too. You know Drew, don't you?"

Hilda beamed. "Of course, I do. I've been in his gallery many a time."

Drew bowed slightly. "It's always a pleasure."

Woody arrived with two drinks of some sparkling beverage. He handed one to his mother. Another round of pleasantries was exchanged, then Drew, Rocky, and Terry ambled over to the bar to fetch bevvies.

Hilda stared after Rocky. "I can't believe how much he looks like his father."

Rose looked at the floor. "Yes. Some days I even call him Trey by accident."

"If he'd just been a little faster hitting that silent alarm button..." Woody trailed off.

PC straightened her shoulders. "Excuse me?"

Woody closed his eyes and let out a breath. "That was an incredibly stupid thing to say. I'm sorry."

Well, this isn't at all awkward. Still, PC managed to smile up at Woody. "You look good. How are you feeling?"

"I'm getting there. Thanks."

PC nodded. "Good. I'm glad. It was hard to see... I'm glad you're better."

A faint smile bowed Woody's lips. "So, I hear you're retired now."

"Yep."

"I got you a ginger ale." Drew handed PC a water glass full of bubbly gold liquid.

"Thanks."

PC was also thankful that the awkward small talk was interrupted, but she sensed tension between Drew and Woody. Fortunately, Hiro and Annie joined the party.

"Oh, honey, you look so beautiful!" Rose crooned. "When is the wedding?"

"We recommend against the holidays—those are already stressful enough." Simone Reynolds appeared out of nowhere. Her blonde hair was swept into an updo decorated with tiny silk roses.

"Please," Caitlyn, who had come up on the other side of PC, added. "Let us host your wedding."

Hiro's eyes swept the expensive venue.

Caitlyn shook her finger like a windshield wiper. "Unh uh. It will be our treat. To try to make up for the engagement fiasco."

"Besides," Simone beamed at Hiro. "We owe you for catching the poisoner. As long as she was roaming free, people weren't going to believe it wasn't the oysters, no matter what the Health Department said."

Hiro's eyes locked on PC's. "Actually, it was—"

She cut him off. "Hiro, you did a fabulous job. You deserve all the credit."

Caitlyn and Simone led the engaged couple away, presumably to discuss wedding packages.

Woody glared at PC. "I know you've been doing your own investigations behind my back with Tran."

"He consulted me. I was happy to help."

"Consulting… Why don't you come to my office next week and we'll discuss your over-active curiosity?"

I'd rather not. "Sure. When?"

"Just call first and make sure I'm there."

"I'm starving. Where's the food?" Justice broke in.

"This way. Follow me, ladies." Drew linked his arm with PC's.

There was no sit-down meal, just crystal plates and finger foods. At the dessert end of the buffet, PC saw little tartlets filled with chocolate mousse and a little rosette of whipped cream. They were adorable.

But she couldn't bring herself to eat one.

If you enjoyed this book, please consider leaving a review at your favorite book site. Reviews help other readers find and enjoy new books!

Other books by Holly Dey:

Large Print Editions

Manor of Death: The Possumwood Mysteries Large Print Edition Book 1

Death on the Half Shell: The Possumwood Mysteries Large Print Edition Book 2

Azalea Trail of Death: The Possumwood Mysteries Large Print Edition Book 3

Death Re-Enacted: The Possumwood Mysteries Large Print Edition Book 4

Death Rides a Bobcat: The Possumwood Mysteries Large Print Edition Book 5

Key to Death: The Possumwood Mysteries Large Print Edition Book 6

Death Curated: The Possumwood Mysteries Large Print Edition Book 7

Pool of Death: The Possumwood Mysteries Large Print Edition Book 8

All Death No Cattle: The Possumwood Mysteries Large Print Edition Book 9

Death is Lager than Life: The Possumwood Mysteries Large Print Edition Book 10

Art of Death: The Possumwood Mysteries Large Print Edition Book 11

Little Town of Death-Lehem: The Possumwood Mysteries Large Print Edition Book 12